HELL'S HEROES

John Gordon

ISBN 978-1-78222-827-1

Cover photos: Pixabay: GidonPico; Sammy-Williams

Book design, layout and production management by Into Print www.intoprint.net

+44 (0)1604 832149

For the lads

At the beginning we had all been sworn to secrecy, this was never to be spoken about outside of the group. After 35 years I feel I can now tell my story as it happened. This is the first time I or anyone from the ground has spoken about any of the tasks my unit had to endure. What you will read is based on my personal experiences in the armed forces. Some fact, some fiction. Out of my respect for the men I served with I have kept names accurate and true to character. It is up to you to decide what you take away from this, even what is true, but before you do, read my story. Go and talk to a veteran who has had a similar past to mine. You'll find their stories more exhilarating than what you could watch at the cinema, more heartbreaking than the saddest of love songs and which show no greater proof of honour, sacrifice and respect for man.

This is part one of my story.

Prologue

My swollen eyes were burning. The pale moonlight offered little fortune and mixed with dirt, blood and sweat had taken visibility from my favour. Each painful blink seemed to only bring back a sliver of reality. Like a slideshow of how things can go from bad to worse. The smell of decay clung to the stifling air. It was as though the shallow graves of the men who had fallen before us were calling for new bedfellows.

The warm breath of Kenny and Brit filled my senses. They stood to my right, as they always had, which seemed to make the situation worse. They had been my brothers through thick and thin. I had fought with them, laughed and cried with them and now I was going to die with them. I couldn't protect them from this as I had with so many encounters in our time in service.

Big Bob and his fucked-up disciples drew nearer to us. The sound of their heavy footsteps breaking the dry twigs and fallen leaves was followed by their heavier taunts and sneers. They wanted us to know they were close. Wanted our minds to feel as broken as our bodies, and they didn't give a shit how loud they were or how loud they could make us scream. We were alone out here. Alone in the middle of God knows where but not even God himself could help us now.

The last two and a half months in the Falklands, I thought I'd seen everything. I'd felt every emotion and my head and heart had grown as calloused and hard as my fists. But this wasn't war, not some kind of exercise, this was a *hunt*. Cruel, and with none of the honour we deserved. We were the crippled mice waiting for the hungry cat to finish us off.

I turned to Kenny and then to Brit. They didn't look the way I felt. Brit held a branch studded with the nails he'd salvaged from the fire pit at our holding brig whilst Kenny tightened his grip on the dagger he had made, tied with the cord he'd taken from the rotten piss-stained mattress we were forced to sleep on for days. My glance met theirs: "We got this Geordie" Brit said followed with a split-second bloodstained grin. I turned back to the small opening of dirt we had found refuge in. A familiar copper taste filled my mouth. A taste I'd become overly accustomed to over the last few days. My teeth gripped my bottom lip splitting the flimsy scab that had barely formed since my last beating. Blood flowed down my throat and as it fell ignited the fire in my belly. Brit was right, this wasn't the end. I wouldn't let it end like this. Not after everything I'd done. Every obstacle I had overcome. Everything I'd ever worked towards had fallen apart.

I'd felt through my young life I wouldn't amount to much. I had signed up to serve my country the day after my nineteenth birthday, and after working harder than I believed I was capable of, despite the beatings from the army lads, my dyslexia, the training that hammered every fibre of my being, in four years I'd become something. I'd developed into a man I was proud to wear the skin of and I'd be damned if I was going to let men who were less than half the worth of me take that away. "You're right Brit," I said; *"We've fucking got this!"*

1: The Family

There are moments in life where a second can last a lifetime. A single heartbeat pumps more life into your body than the one before. As I stood locked in entropy, my clenched fists gripped as tightly as my jaw, I remembered what all of this was worth. One blink faded my vista to black, the next broke the laws of science and took me six years ago to the start of this journey.

"Geordie John!" the summoning startled me. I slid from under the '76 Land Rover that had seen much better days. The rear break-pads had been my sole focus for the last hour and any distraction away from this came as a welcome. Like the skin on my fingertips, my patience was starting to wear thin.

"Are you Geordie John Gordon?" asked the lad with a grin, who I knew was Duncan Bustin, or Dunc to his mates. He was a six-foot, thick set lad, not the fittest but I knew him for never giving up on a challenge.

"Aye," I replied in my typical northern charm. His face showed he knew quite well who I was. I looked up at him sensing that something was going on.

"The BSM wants you in his office," Dunc barked, attempting to once again hold back his overly apparent grin.

I got up and started to put the tools away.

"You haven't got time for that" he told me. "You need to go straight away."

I pushed the tools under the Land Rover with my left foot and started walking towards the hangar doors, wiping my hands on my coveralls as I went. There wasn't anyone else to be seen or heard. Like a curtain had been pulled across this section of the base. Dunc was walking a step or two behind me. I still had this bad feeling I wasn't going to enjoy this distraction.

Just as I turned the corner to leave the hangar – BANG!

I went down like a bag of shit. Brit, a man I knew only by reputation, had caught me from the other side of the door right in the guts and at the same time Dunc had taken to my rear and got a heavy jab to my kidneys.

Mark Britnal was a Cockney from the west end of London. I had always felt he wanted to test me. He was a bit of a show off, always challenging himself with fights in the town and in the local villages. I remember seeing him one night take out two locals when they tried to get the pool table from some younger army lads. I say the young ones, they were about two years younger than him, 18 or 19 maybe. But Brit was having none of it. He sat on the end of the table and as the two local lads approached him he gave two clean punches, one to each face, and down they went. The first one he hit, his nose popped like a water balloon; Claret all over the floor. That was a shock to everyone, but Brit just got off the table and said to the young army lads, "Start playing pool boys, the table's yours now." Not even looking back at the two lads on the floor. I was impressed by his strength back then but I didn't appreciate it right now.

I hit the floor, struggling to get my breath. I looked up at them in agony.

As I was getting up I saw a third stepping up to take a

turn – Chris Catton, a well-built lad who looked as though he could handle himself, had started to walk towards me saying to Brit and Dunc, "The Geordie isn't as tough as he looks, is he?" That was the point I decided to go for it. I had to make a stand. I couldn't let them get the better of me. If I did it would be like school all over again. Me having to fight every day just so the lads had a bit entertainment at break times. Just as I was in the half up position I hit Dunc with a punch right under the chin, sending him back over and down on his ass. Brit came for me grinning, like my defence wouldn't be much more than another facet to exaggerate when telling the boys in the dinner hall, how the 'Geordie' tried to get the better of him. There was no time for me to decide whether he was going to strike or not. My foot came up, and I side-kicked him in the gut, doubling him around it. I could see Chris out of the corner of my eye. A spinning round house kick to the head put him on his backside. None of them were aware I was a black belt at karate. I started training after leaving school. I had to start to stick up for myself. Being bullied there had been enough and within five years I'd gained my black belt and had even made it to the UK under-21 team.

At this point Dunc was getting back up to his feet. "You're a mad Geordie twat. We're only messing with you."

Knowing I couldn't let them get the better of me I replied, "So was I. Now does the B.S.M. want to see me?"

"No, you mad git!" Dunc responded.

As I turned to walk back to the Land Rover I saw some of the other lads had been watching. Paul Donahue (Donny to his mates) was one of them. He had a strong profile, large build and stoic presence. The sort you could probably hit all day and he wouldn't flinch before you wore yourself out. He walked up to me. I thought he would be the one that would put me in my place, but no, he just said,

"Nice one Geordie, I don't think you will get any more trouble from them, but watch your back, because some of the other lads will want to have a go."

Donny was the cool quiet type, didn't say a lot, but took it all in, and when the time was right, you would find out just what he was all about. One lad that understood this was Tommo. He would try to antagonize anyone. We had gone in the mess hall one day just for a pie and a cuppa and Tommo thought he would start with Donny; he gave him all kinds of verbal. Donny just sat chatting with the lads ignoring it. Tommo went in harder and started pushing him with all the insults that could be said about his family and where he lived, but still not even a flinch from Donny. If it had been me, I would have put him on his backside. We all waited for him to snap; the atmosphere was cold, everyone felt the eerie chill, but Donny got up and just walked out, not saying a word.

The next day when we went on parade, the Troop Sgt informed us, Tommo was missing. As it turned out he was in hospital; what happened we never found out, but Tommo was pretty quiet after that.

As the time after my attack passed, the time spent looking over my shoulder grew shorter. I stopped sleeping with one eye open and being paranoid about the sour taste in my food. It seemed I had been accepted by the regiment as not someone to fuck with. Word had got around that I had put Brit on his ass, and it seemed that was what had to happen. You stand up for yourself and you got respect. It wasn't about being the big man on base, the tough one, the crazy one. Just another man that will not take shit and won't back down. A hard lesson that undeniably was very necessary. If only I had done this at school, how different life would have been for me.

I made some very close friends, Kenny Dinsdale was one of the best. We went through training together and got on really well. He was a boxer from Hartlepool, the 'Pocket Rocket' I called him, small but fast. When we get together we started to do some extra fitness training in the gym, after we had completed all of the block jobs. We had to complete all our duties before we got our heads down or phone home, or do anything else you fancied. One thing we couldn't do was leave camp, that was a big no, not until you had completed the first eight weeks training.

One day while we did a bit extra training, he asked me to do a bit of sparring with him. We didn't do a lot of sparring as I did my karate and he got on with his boxing, but me being the friendly and helpful person I am, I agreed.

What could go wrong? What indeed, he was hitting me with punches that seemed to be coming from an endless line of fists. Anytime he took a step back he just smiled then started another on slort, I was not having this, so up came the foot, flashed past his head and came back with a slap on the forehead. That stopped him; he knew that we were the same. We just left it at that and never tried to be the one in control. Kenny was part of 9 battery, and somehow got to work in the gym just after he arrived at the regiment, the job I had always dreamed of. I would go down to see him at times, and he fitted in well with the lads there, Tony Watt and Glen Harwood, both with the shared mentality as Kenny. I would go into the gym, the office being at the bottom end, so any trip there required a walk through the main gym hall. Getting in was ok but getting out was a different matter. Every time you went in the gym there was a different challenge but it was always the same rule, you got out if you could avoid getting hit with a dart, javelin, or any object that they could find to throw at you.

One day I went in and it was all quiet, not a typical day as you always heard something going on. Halfway through the gym and I found out why – an ambush. One of them had seen me coming down the road, so decided to have a little fun. I was attacked by all three: Glen got me with a pole, Kenny had a skipping rope, and Tony golf balls. I was hit from all directions. One of the golf balls hit me in the centre of my spine; the pain shot though me like a knife being lunged though my skin. Once I went down, that was it, my eyes tightly closed, trying to shut out the pain. I was tied up and laid into, *all in good fun* as they informed me. Not fun for me, but now I was starting to get the sense of humour of the army, well, it certainly was the humour of the regiment: work hard, play hard, and *be* hard; you do that and you will fit in. I knew one day I would get them back, the three of them had the name Gym Queens – it should have been Gym *Animals*. I did get revenge, one at a time I got them back, but I knew it would not stop at that. These guys would always have the last laugh.

Glen and Tony turned out to be top lads, but the 'banter' as they called it continued. We all turned out to be the best of mates, and I knew if I was in need of help anywhere or any time, I just had to pick up the phone and one of them would be there. That is why we got the name from other regiments as 'The Family.'

2: War

It was Easter 1982, we had all been knocked off for the holidays and I was going home to visit my family. I knew the traffic would be busy though the village, so I decided to walk down to get a paper and give the traffic time to clear.

It was a beautiful day, bright but cool, it was days like today that you really had the chance to appreciate being in your civvies, no overalls, rigid uniform just some well-worn jeans and white T-shirt that had seen better days. The village square was quiet, and the trees glittering in the sunlight. As I walked back to the camp, I was thinking of the two weeks ahead. Going out for a drink or two, catching up with all the Gordons I hadn't realised I actually missed and seeing my best mate Dave McGlen.

Before I joined the army. We had done most things together, we met at about 5 years old, my mam and his were best friends, so that was how it all started. We went through school together, we joined the A.T.C. together, and even started Karate together. Dave was really good at Karate, even having the chance to represent England under 21s. He got a job as a mechanic and was settled. I felt a little jealous at his content life but the more I thought about it the more I knew I wasn't ready for that yet. The army was in me from a kid and it never changed. I enjoyed the skills I was building. School left me unfulfilled and I thought I couldn't make it anywhere, but I was. The hard days at the beginning at the barracks I even seemed to look back on fondly. It had made me laugh out loud as I pictured Dave's face as I went through 'Geordie Gordon's' early days.

As I got passed the last house coming out of the village, a motorbike pulled up alongside me. "You Geordie Gordon?" the voice from under the helmet asked.

"Yes. Why?"

"You are requested to go straight to the guard room, as we are going to war."

I grinned at him. Who he was I didn't know at the time, but he was right. However, I had no intention of going to the guard room as he had said. I was just going to head home assuming the joker in a helmet was someone Brit or Kenny had sent down to wind me up.

I was walking past the camp gates and a voice called out,

"GORDON! Get your arse over here!" It was the R.S.M (Regiment Sergeant Major) Richard Malaka. He was stood at the gate. "I need you to go around all of the houses on the estate over there" as he pointed to the houses opposite the cam "and inform all staff to report to their battery office A.S.A.P. And take notes of the house numbers, so we can check the ones that try to ignore you."

"Yes Sir, what will I tell them if they ask?"

His face never flinched as he said the words I never thought I'd hear in my time in service:

"We are going to war."

Shit. Shit! I couldn't think clear! My head was spinning and my mouth was dry. My body was driving my legs in a direction my head had no control over. I just had to get to my room, pick up my gear and do what I was instructed.

The next hour I still remember as a blur, I knew nothing

more than the last words my R.S.M had said. The same questions spinning in my head were asked by everyone I spoke to. Who were we going to war with? How were we going to get to the war area? And am I ready for this?

I rang home as soon as I had a chance. I told my dad.

"You keep your head down son, and come back home in one piece. Don't tell your mam, leave that to me," he said.

As I was heading back to the camp, soldiers were running past me with their full packs on. When I returned I gave the R.S.M. the list as he had asked for.

I was sent to my battery offices. I would be given instruction from my Battery Sergeant Major what was going to happen now.

We went to the Falklands the next day. It lasted 74 days. 255 British soldiers lost their lives. My regiment was very lucky, we lost no men, and only had one lad that lost his arm, Kipper, he was a good friend of Kenny's, and turned out to be a very good friend of mine.

The Falklands had taken a lot form us, we had seen things lads our age possibly never should. Some had to put up with some unbelievable weather conditions; you would hear some of them crying in their scratcher and some praying. It was hard, but as one of the old hands had said, 'This was war, and not a game like exercise we had been on; we had signed up for this so we had to get on with it.'

When we were returned to camp life felt different, like we had returned somewhere we only vaguely remembered from a dream. The normality of violence everyday changes you. To live on the edge for so long made normal life seem not quite right. It was safe to say that after any time on duty we needed a slow introduction back into normality.

3: Real Life

After the first days back, the R.S.M. got the regiment on the parade square. He gave us the usual spiel, what a good job we had done, and how proud he was of us all. All of us could have a night on the town before we could head off home on leave. This was if we didn't get into any trouble and he was happy we had adapted ok. Three days had passed and we got the all clear to hit the town, there was about 10 of us that went to Lincoln, the normal place we drank was Scunthorpe, but we knew most of the lads would be heading down there and they would be looking for some locals to ease back to real life with. My battery just wanted a quiet night, in the army there was never a quite night out with the lads, but as quiet as it could be. So off we went, hit a few of the bars then off to the night club.

The night was just as we hoped it would be. Drinks were getting sent over to us with compliments, everyone was giving us cheers, 'Heroes' they called us. D.J's were calling out all night, "Thank the heroes!" The drinks just kept coming. Me and the lads just kept knocking them back.

I took it upon myself to look out for everyone as I knew some of them would go overboard with all the appreciation Lincoln offered, and they did. The night was a good one, everyone was happy, no trouble. Kenny and Brit got well pissed, they could hardly stand, this was the time we knew we were ready to head back. I paid a visit to the gents and when I returned I had lost Kenny and Brit, talking to some slappers I thought. I weaved around the club still catching some high fives and handshakes from the locals but I was starting to get a bit frustrated, I was tired and ready to leave. I headed to the exit, the lads must be waiting outside I thought.

On my way I saw Donny, Dunc, Tony and Glen chatting with some lasses. They stood by a large unframed painting of a disfigured face with parts of the skull visible, bleeding through its eye sockets, something a bit sinister for a place designed to cater good times but like most 'art', I didn't get it. Chris had said he was off to stay with a lass he had picked up, so I continued to head outside.

Kenny and Brit were not there, they were nowhere to be seen. I knew they must have left the club, I had been in the gents and wove around the club in a strategic search vector to catch them, so they must be out here somewhere.

Outside the fresh air hit me hard, I thought I held back on the pints but the cool late summer air proved me wrong. I headed as best I could to the side of the club to see if they were taking a slash or asking folk where the nearest chippy was. On my way I saw two doormen run past me the opposite way toward the lane at the other side of the club. I didn't think anything of it and just continued to search the front area for them. I knew they couldn't be far away as they could hardly stand. A young lass came running from the back lane the bouncers had disappeared down. Tears ran down her face which disturbed the heavy layer of make-up she wore. She sobbed to her friend, *"The bouncers have two lads in the lane and are giving them a good kicking, I think they will kill them if no one stops them!"*

The penny dropped, I knew it was the lads who were going to be at the other end of the bouncer's punches, so I ran straight around looking for Brit and Kenny.

The two of them were on the floor and the boots were flying into them. There were four bouncers around them, kicking the shit out of them. Kenny was out of it, and I could hear Brit shouting "I WILL FUCK THE LOT OF YOU WHEN I GET UP!"

Two of the bouncers saw me coming and headed for me. One of them was a prat, I could see he was not a fighter, he was a follower, the sort that lets his mate do all the fighting and he was the one that will hit you when you are on the ground. I went straight for him, I had to dodge the big lad to get to him, straight in the balls with the first kick I put him straight to the floor. The second lad was the big one, I put one straight on the nose, blood poured straight down his face, splats of it hit me on the cheek and the warmth of the blood felt good. I had never felt that feeling before, pleasure in violence, but I did now and it sobered me up as the adrenalin fired through my body. As he went back wobbling I started laying into him. I felt his nose crack under my fist and with every punch to his face I felt more and more release. All the fights I had been made to have as a kid and all kickings I got at school when I was bullied, just seemed to come flooding back. But now I was not scared, every punch felt good. He was unsteady, but he wouldn't go down. I took my eye off the ball thinking how I could drop him when a third hit me from behind.

Kenny was still out of it and now Brit had followed suit. Brit had taken the hardest of the beatings but Kenny seemed to have come off the worst. His face was a mess. I fell to the floor and as I started to get back up. I turned and all four of the men turned all attention to me. It was the hardest beating of my life. "Get the van" I heard between punches. As I lay there drifting into unconsciousness, I felt less and less pain in my body and tried my hardest to listen to what the bouncers were saying.

"Bob will love these ones, real fighters these dicks," 'the prat' said.

"They better last longer than the last fucking squaddies we got!" said another.

I knew something bad was coming but I had no strength to do anything about it I felt my body being lifted, it felt euphoric for a moment but it was quickly replaced when my back was greeted by a cold slap to a hard surface. The cool air was replaced with the stale smell of dust, piss and mildew. I heard a heavy metal door slide shut then a distant garble of low pitched voices. I couldn't open my eyes so for a moment I let them rest.

As I began to come around it took a while to work out if my eyes were open or closed. Slowly as my eyes adjusted I made out that I was in the back of a van. The windows had been boarded up and the only light came from the windscreen in the front driver's section. Kenny and Brit were in there with me. And so was one more, but this figure was sat upright with a small halo of street light glowing from his shaved head. He jumped to his feet and grabbed the back of my head, slammed my face into the floor of the van, the pain ran down my spine and I felt my top lip split, the blood trickle down my left cheek on to the van floor, it must be a bad one as the hole of my cheek warmed up as the blood spread around it.

"SQUADDIE PRICK! YOU THINK YOU'RE A BIG HARD MAN EH?" he shouted in my ear. I said nothing. He tied my hands behind my back and then moved down to do the same to my legs.

My face had landed toward Kenny, he was in a bad way, still unconscious and his face ripped to shreds. Both of his eyes were up like puddings, blood starting to clog his nostrils where his nose had popped. He wouldn't be to see out of one eye for some time, that was for definite. I could hear Brit was starting to come around to. I had to keep him quiet, he was the sort that would never say die, so I had to convince him to let me think.

"What you gonna do with us?" I asked the man trying to mask Brit's movements with the sound of our conversation.

"Gonna have a little trip lads, take you some place nice and play a few games" he sneered. Brit kept quiet, if he was awake I knew he'd be in doing his best to get up and take on our captor. As he finished tying up my legs he moved to Brit. I turned my head and could see Brit's eyes were closed. I turned back to Kenny whose mouth had fallen open from the clogged blood in his nostrils. His two front teeth were gone. Although he was a mess, I knew he would be ok, fighting was fun to him. Back in Hartlepool, him and his brother Rob would go out looking for a fight and if they lost, mind that was not often, but when they did they would laugh about it as they staggered home.

"Where are you gonna take us?" I asked.

"SHUT UP YOU GEORDIE CUNT! I'M NOT TELLING YOU NOTHING!" he spat back.

One last try I thought to get any information I could.

"Look we can sort this out, if you tell—"

He had tightly grabbed my hair in his hand at the back of my head and smacked me back down to floor of the van.

My face was hot, my mouth dry … and then there was nothing.

4: The Road

I woke. My body felt like I had fallen down a cliff and hit every rock on the way. My eyes blurred as they adjusted to the dim light. The van was moving now, I didn't know for how long. Pins and needles were numbing my hands and feet where they were bound but using my head I forced my back to arch for levity to try sit up. My entire strength was needed just to pull up my knees to my abdomen and then to raise my head and shoulders from the floor. After a few moments to recover I looked to the lads. Only the three of us were in the back of the van now. There were no signs of a door handle from the inside of our cage. Obviously to keep us in here. The small window which lead to the front section of the van had bars across it and the glass was frosted. It didn't reveal anything but the quick burst of light from a passing street light.

I couldn't hear any other traffic on the road, and the road surface felt uneven and poorly maintained we must be somewhere pretty remote.

Kenny started to come around, I inched over to him and using my feet to lift his shoulders I somehow managed to get him up. Brit meanwhile was starting to wriggle and used the wheel shelf to pull himself up. They both looked like shit. I stared at their bloody faces and tried my best to quietly explain what had happened and what I thought was going to happen. They sat quietly, trying to figure a way out of this.

The silence brought no ideas so we sat in disbelief. They couldn't believe it, things like this just don't happen, that was what we all thought – but it was and we had to deal with it.

Kenny in his typical northern attitude was the first to break the long silence.

"I can use this as part of my S.A.S. training."

That was his dream, to join the SAS. I turned to Kenny, his toothless grin failed to lift the heavy atmosphere.

"This *isn't* training Kenny. These fuckers are bringing us out her to execute or torture us. We have no weapons or gear. We're gonna have to try negotiating our way out of this one." As soon as the words left my lips I realised how stupid I sounded. These guys were not going to entertain us with a negotiation. Unless they were delivering us back to the barracks to get our arses smacked we have gone beyond the point of forgive and forget. Brit piped in to keep us calm,

"I think Geordie is right mate, we have to sort this out in the right way."

We couldn't get the ropes untied from our hands, so we decided to sit back and think.

The van swung a tight right knocking us all over to our sides. There was movement and soon after the sound of two doors opening and slamming followed. The outside handle creaked as it was turned, and the back of the van opened. The fresh air was welcoming. Outside was pitch black, the moon was low and I just caught a glimpse of a thick tree line until torchlight illuminated 'the prat' that I had put on his backside outside the club and another I didn't recognise. The prat got in and started to lay into me, as he did he kept on saying,

"A Geordie and a war hero? You're a BIG SOFT SHIT!"

I turned my head to one side to save my face, the punches rained down on the side of my head, *fuck* it was hurting like hell, but I just had to sit and take it. One of the other lads pulled him off me.

"Get back in the front and keep it down, we don't want to get caught *you dick!*"

They locked us back in; Kenny and Brit started to see this was not a game.

Kenny asked what had happened to the rest of the lads, I informed them: Chris had picked up a lass, and the rest were still in the club when I came out looking for them. No one saw us being taken, maybe the lass who had seen Kenny and Brit getting beat up could have told them but that was our only lifeline. I didn't care much for those odds.

We were alone out here and *nobody* was looking for us.

5: Clues

The night had been what everyone needed. No one can remember a better one to get the feeling of normal life back. The burnt onions, greasy burgers and fluorescent yellow cheese was a welcome smell and sight. Even Shelia, the semi-bearded, non-gender specific burger van operator was a vision of beauty when Tony, Glen and Dunc left the club.

Tony was the first to wonder where we had gone. Dunc had said to just leave us, laughing that we'd be having a skinny dip in the Witham but Tony was like me, always trying to keep the lads together and safe. He went back into the club but couldn't find us. On his way back out one of the doormen asked if he had lost his boyfriend. He could take a joke but now wasn't the time.

"The army lads I came with. Have you seen them mate?"

The doorman just grinned, "Don't worry too much, they'll be having a lovely time. I'm sure they'll be back soon mate." The doorman turned and walked deeper into the entrance to the club. Tony thought his reply was strange but didn't think too much of it at the time. *Typical meathead prick* Tony thought. He went back outside to see Glen and Dunc and now the rest of the lads were out and by the burger van. He spoke to Donny, as he always observed what was going on around him; Donny hadn't seen anything. Then to each of the other lads he asked the same. The general conclusion was we got pissed, got some chips and headed back to the barracks. Tony thought they were probably right so they all headed back to get some sleep and hear all the funny stories in the morning.

The van was moving again, we were trying to feel the movement, what direction it was travelling and the turns it was taking. It was not long before we gave up. We had been in the van for about an hour and a half that we knew of but longer while we were all unconscious. We must have gone onto the motorway, which direction we couldn't tell. Kenny asked me to try again to loosen the ropes around his hands. As I tried Brit was trying to think strategy.

"If we can't get the ropes loose, we need to stay calm when they get us out of the van."

I couldn't get the ropes loose and I could feel my hands starting to swell up with the rope being so tight. Kenny's eye was getting more swollen, he couldn't open it and it looked as if it would be like that for days. I could feel we had gone off the motorway and started to travel a lot slower.

"When they get us out, one of two things is going to happen. One, they will start to lay into us again or they will look at us and think any more of a kicking and there will be no fun with us. They will need us at least half alive," Kenny added.

"OK Kenny, if this is right, you and Brit look like shit and need to *act* like it. No matter what happens, *don't* retaliate, I mean that lads! I know what you're both like, never say die, and I respect that but at this moment, you have to wait until the time is right." It was a tough thing to say to the lads as I knew their characters; they didn't like to act or show weakness but the alternative is we would not have any chance to recover our strength.

The movement of the van felt as if it started to go on to a dirt track, and Kenny told us to get ready for what might be heading in our direction. Brit moved towards me, I thought he was going to say something to me but no – he stuck the nut on the bridge of my nose.

"There," he said. "*You* now look like shit as well."

My nose split open and I could feel it starting to swell straightaway.

"Geordie, Brit is right, you needed that," said Kenny.

I could see they looked like shit, and I felt like it, but I must have looked a lot better than they did.

We must have travelled about three to four miles on dirt track when we came to a halt. We all seemed to take a deep breath at the same time, expecting the worst. As the two doors at the front of the van opened then slammed shut again, one of the men opened the back doors. He looked at us and said,

"Piss break lads, do you want one?"

Kenny piped up, "Yes please, can you stay where you are, so I can piss in your face you dickhead."

The man just laughed.

"You can try later cocksucker. You're the one I'm gonna be after later and when I catch you and beat the crap out of you I'll piss on your corpse and remember what you just said." He slammed the door and was still laughing as he walked away to have his piss.

I was mad at Kenny. I stared at him and felt my face start to burn.

"What the fuck are you playing at? You need to keep your mouth *SHUT*!"

"Yes," said Brit, "because he *is* going to piss in it!"

I was trying to be serious, but we all had a bit giggle, trying to keep the noise down so they couldn't hear us.

"I wasn't trying to piss him off Geordie," said Kenny. "Did you not hear what he said? *When I catch you.* These fuckers are taking us out to be hunted."

The laughter stopped. Kenny had got us at least one answer to what the men were planning to do with us. All I could think of was if Kenny was right, we were being taken out into the middle of nowhere to be used in a hunt.

We could hear them chatting at the side of the van as they pissed. "How far now?" 'the prat' said. "About 25 minutes to the holding shed" said the other. They got back in the van, and off we went again, this time we must have travelled for about an hour before we stopped again – so much for the 25 minutes I thought. We heard one of them say, "Let me do the talking, and you keep off the lads in the back. If Big Bob sees you giving them any sort of shit he will have you."

The door to the back of the van opened and two of them looked in at us.

"This is where the fun starts lads, and we are going to have a lot of it with you three, I bet you wish you had your mates with you now."

The one that had got in the back of the van at the night club, was the one that got in the van now, and his mate called out to him, in a quiet voice,

"Don't touch them Steve, you heard what Peter said."

I worked out the one that was happy to lay into me and Kenny when I was out of it, was Steve. That was good to know because if we do get out of this mess, I was going to be the first one to sort him out. The prat was Peter.

The van doors remained open and Steve and Peter stood

watching us while periodically checking their watches. My lip was still stinging from him slamming my face into the van floor. I was nursing it the best I could when a third lad came up to the doorway. I hadn't seen this one before, he looked at us but never spoke a word. He moved over to Steve and Peter and appeared to talk with them though I couldn't hear a word he spoke. The sound of a vehicle approached and grew louder until its headlights filled the back of the van, blinding us from what was now happening outside.

"Here's Bob" I heard one say. Bob, they had mentioned him before, maybe he was the boss? Organiser? Probably the one Peter sticks his nose up the arse the most to. A break in the headlights cast a shadow of relief on my face. Big Bob I assumed, and he *was* big, about 6ft 4in and built like a brick shithouse. So now there was four of them, Big Bob, the boss, Steve the shithead, the one that was happy to hit you when you are out of it, Peter 'the prat', one that was out there for the cash, and the last one whose name I hadn't heard yet but didn't say a lot. I couldn't work out if he was just a quiet one or was not into this sort of stuff but had been dragged along with it all. Bob looked at the three of us,

"I think we can make a quid or two from this lot. I'll inform the right doormen from around the circle, I know a lot of them love to break the army lads. That should keep the three of them on the run for three or four days. Put them in the shed over there for now." The three men nodded and started to move to Bob's car boot, I assumed to get some gear to keep us in line. Bob stood a moment longer then moved around with them. He spoke loud and I heard him tell the men,

"I will get contacting the packs to put the word out, I can

then arrange a date for the hunt to start, in the meantime Pete, get your lads to get some food for them and get that van out of sight, put it in the barn for now. Get the new plates on and give it a once over. Billy take Steve with you and get what you think we will need for a week, there's a grand in the duffle. If we need more or other supplies we can get the lads on the way in to pick up some."

So, Billy was the quiet one, he was younger than the other men, just a teenager. His eyes never locked on ours but there was something familiar about him.

Kenny and Brit were staring at me when I turned toward them. Their faces hit me hard. I gave them an uncomfortable smile in reassurance.

My belly was in knots and head was spinning with all that I just digested in my ears. They spoke about us like cattle to a farmer. I understood in this moment that words would not serve us now. Big Bob didn't regard us with any respect. We were meat, plain and simple, heading to slaughter.

I bit my tongue not to say the words I truly felt. But we were fucked.

6: The Shed

We had a good look around as they dragged us to the shed, nothing for miles but heather and long grass. The landscape was all up and down and tufts of grass all around, quite a lot like the Falklands. I knew if they were letting us run off from here we would have to watch our step. We only had on dress shoes, no grips to speak of, and not combat boots. We wore out smart trousers and shirts, nothing which could really protect us from the elements.

Next to the shed were two barn type buildings, one had the door open; inside, were two old cars. The other building looked as if it was locked. As they pulled us into the shed I could see a stove, one old chair that was in the far-left corner and two old, mildew covered piss-stained mattresses in the middle. This was going to be home for a day or two I thought. They pushed me to the floor by the mattresses, Brit was put on one of the mattresses, and Kenny was left in the middle on the floor.

I was starting to feel for him, his eyes shut with the swelling, blood had dried over them and he could hardly breathe though his nose due to the swelling, congealed blood and snot. Steve pushed him, he hit the floor head first and I felt it. Brit called out,

"YOU BASTARDS! You'll be sorry for this!"

Bob shouted in as he was walking to the locked barn,

"Untie them, they can't get out and they need to have a bit

strength in them when they try to run off."

Steve looked a bit scared, he must be thinking we will try to have a go at them; not a chance at the moment. We didn't have a clue where we were, Kenny and Brit wouldn't be able to make 10 feet, never mind miles. As Steve started to untie my feet, I looked him in the eyes. Will I have a go at you? I thought, there are only two of you now mate. I could see Steve looking for backup from Billy.

Billy looked back at him, "How do you want to do this Steve?"

"I don't know," he replied.

I had a feeling neither of them had done this before.

"I might have a go at you Steve," I said. "I can scream out, pretend you have stuck one on me Steve, and Big Bob will have you, remember he said not to harm us."

Brit laughed at him and said; "You had better stick one on us now because when we get out you'll need to pray that I don't get you."

Steve started to go red in the face, he was not happy being in the shed with us, and not having his mates with him. Billy told us to fill up on fruits and that we wouldn't be getting anything hot to eat. He untied our hands and feet and headed out of the shed. As they got to the door, Billy turned back and looked at us with sadness in his eyes, "I'm not into this sort of stuff, just so you know." He shut the doors and I could hear chains and a padlock being fastened to the door.

It had to be about 4 o'clock in the morning, as the sun was starting to come up, Kenny made his way over to the mattresses and sat down beside me and Brit.

"Well lads, it's pretty cosy isn't it? No Holiday Inn but the staff are nice." He smiled the best he could and said with a sigh as he rubbed his wrists "What do you think is going to happen to us now?"

I looked at the two of them and couldn't say a word, then Brit looked up and said, "I have heard of this sort of thing happening when I was back in London, before I joined up. I thought it was just scare tactics from my mates to stop me from signing up but I heard the outcome is not good if we get caught. The best thing we can do for now is get some sleep."

Kenny was furious. "GET SOME SLEEP you headcase! Are you for real? I was joking about the Holiday Inn thing you know! We are about to be hunted down like fox mate and you think we should sleep!"

But Brit was right. "Listen, listen," he said, "we can go out of here rested and with clear heads, so we can think straight … or be knackered and all over the place and get caught straight away. That will be the end for us, and by the way mate, you can't even *see*!"

Kenny's face grew fiercer as he shouted with his wounded pride. "I can see enough to look after myself and well enough to see a couple of pussies who don't wanna take a chance for an escape now when they don't expect one!"

"*KENNY!*" I forced out while trying to keep calm, "I *agree* with you. You can take care of yourself even if you were blind. But we'd be stupid to try anything now. So, if we get out, where do we run? Which direction? They have dragged us here for a reason, it's quiet and remote. Exposure would get us maybe before Bob and his men would." I broke off for a moment not wanting to push Kenny off too much. He was as confused and feeling as rotten as me and Brit, so I took my voice down a notch to try make him think different.

"We'll start looking around for anything we can use or take with us and then get to sleep. We'll do as much recon as we can. Listen for any clues to where we are and maybe how to get one of those cars parked next door. We should have at least a day before any more men get here so keep our cool and ears open."

Kenny's face was transfixed on the mattress I was sitting on. I couldn't tell if he agreed with what I said or even listened at all. "You're right Geordie," he quietly said. He moved his way to the corner of the mattress and picked on a piece of frayed stitching. "See if you can find me anything sharp" he said.

I looked at Brit and nodded. The inside of the shed was completely covered in a solid and relatively new metal sheeting. We had no chance of getting out without making a racket. There was a chair in the corner but we couldn't use it because our captors would see any damage to it or if it was missing and put them right onto us. Brit thought different, the chair was an old wooden dining chair with a leather seat pad.

"Don't smash it Brit!" Kenny called out.

"Don't worry I won't," Brit replied.

Kenny continued picking with the mattress. "The beading around the edging, inside of that is a thin cord, I can get it out without them noticing, all I have to do is make a small slit in the trim about four or five times around it and I can pull it out. It's as strong as trip wire this stuff and will choke one of those fuckers no problem."

I stepped on the mattress to look down the wall edging to see if I could find anything. As the mattress sank I remembered it was full of springs and judging by the age of it, would be full of horse hair too. I lifted it up and asked

Kenny to hold it while I took a look under it to see if it was damp. It was, so I turned it over and stood it against a wall. The rotted old fabric tore easily so I ripped a hole in the corner and I was right. I pulled out some of the hair and gave it to Kenny and told him to give some to Brit as we would need it to start a fire later. The spring was a lot harder to get out; I had to twist the wire off that held the others together. As I was working at one end of the mattress, Kenny was at the other pulling out the cord. He was struggling, he could hardly open his eyes, but he wouldn't give up.

I looked over to Brit, he had the chair upside down. On the base was a hessian covering it. Brit ripped it off and stuffed it down his trousers. The base of the chair was also spring loaded, but it had thin metal strips running over the top of them.

"How are you doing?" Kenny asked. "I am just about finished, one more pull and it should be free."

It came out easier than he thought; I still had a bit to do, but would be complete in about five minutes. Kenny called out to Brit, "Is there any metal studs on the bottom of the legs mate?"

Brit turned over the chair and felt around. Much of the fabric had been ripped away or disintegrated but the studs remained. Brit nodded to Kenny.

"Good, we can force them off if the spring is strong enough that Geordie is getting. If we strap them to a tree branch they'll make a mess of the one that comes near us."

Brit and Kenny didn't know each other well, as they were in different batteries at the regiment. They only spoke when we all went out together, but they seemed to be working together well.

"Before you ask lads, the wire that was holding the springs together, we can make snares with them and the springs will help with traps," Brit said. "The sheet of hessian will help with camouflage and the metal strip will slash someone up well. Kenny, I don't need to say what the rope will do."

"Hang the twats, and spring load traps!" Kenny spat.

After about another ten minutes we had everything we could get our hands on. We hid our new weapons well and tried to get our heads down. We all lay on the mattresses and tried to sleep but we couldn't stop thinking about what we were up against and if we would get away from this. To think we all had just returned from the Falklands, not a mark on us and now we were on home soil, battered and bruised.

Nothing made sense, nothing at all.

7: Puzzle pieces

Back at camp Tony got up. As opposed to doing his normal morning routine – a five-mile run to start the day – he decided to head up the corridor to my room. He did this every morning normally *after* the run; he'd put the kettle on and throw some verbal abuse at me in jest – but not today. It was because he knew I would always call into his when I got back from a night on the piss. For a cuppa or to nick his supper. I hadn't so he came to check in and saw that I wasn't there. My bed hadn't been slept in, he knew that there was something wrong.

He went into Brit's room, Brit was also not in, and his bed had not been slept in either. Brit and Dunc shared a room, so Tony gave Dunc a kick.

"Get up mate, have you seen Brit?"

Dunc was not the morning type. His reply was to be expected.

"Piss off and take your head for a shit!"

Tony dragged the quilt off him, and shouted,

"BRIT AND GEORDIE ARE MISSING, GET THE FUCK UP!"

Dunc never worried about anything,

"They will be back before parade, don't worry about it."

Tony didn't think this, he knew I wouldn't stay out and if I did I would have informed him on the night. He went down the corridor to ask Glen and Donny if they had seen us. They hadn't.

"We'll see if Kenny is in the gym," said Glen.

Kenny was in a different battery to the rest of us, he lived in a different block and would be on a different morning parade. Tony would have to wait until he got to the gym for his answers. He was not happy as he could sense something was not right.

All the lads had breakfast and headed to the hangars for parade. Still no sign of the three of us; the B.S.M. Bob Wilson was taking the parade. He was a great bloke, he was hard with us but looked after everyone at the same time. If you got into trouble you would be sorry but he would defend you to the end. He should call out all the names on the parade, but he would just look to see you approach and tick you off the list.

"Where is Gordon, Britnal, and Catton?" he called out. No reply. "Where the hell are they Bustin? You should know as you and Britnal are like a couple! Never apart!"

He was right, the rest of the lads had a good laugh, as we all would. They were like each other's shadow.

"I don't know Sir, they didn't come back last night, I do know Catton picked up a lass and went back to her house, but as for Geordie and Brit we didn't see them after the club," replied Dunc.

"I don't give a shit about Catton, he is getting out so he can go to hell as far as I am concerned, but Brit and Geordie are one of us. After this parade you have *one hour* to find them, and don't come back without them!"

The B.S.M. knew that something was not right. I always would be one of the first on parade and never late. As Bob Wilson was giving the lads the orders for the day, Denis Welsh was walking over with his parade towards ours. He was the B.S.M. for 9 battery that Kenny was in. He called out, "BSM Wilson, have you got Gunner Gordon in your parade? He had a night out with one of my lads and he hasn't returned."

Bob Wilson's eyes flared. "Who would that be Denis? Young Dinsdale, the lad that works in the gym? No I haven't, Gordon and Britnal are also missing."

Tony knew that something had to be wrong, he called out, "Sir can I have a word with you in private please, I think I can help with this." Tony knew something had happened last night and had a bad feeling, he had to find out.

"OK Watt. Down to my office and I will be down soon."

Bob gave out the rest of the jobs for the day to the lads, and dismissed them. Wilson invited Denis to the office as he thought he should hear what Tony had to say.

*

As they walked into the office, Tony was sitting with his head in his hands. Tony stood up and straight away Bob and Denis could see Tony was not right.

"OK Watt, what is it you know?" asked Bob Wilson.

"Well Sir, there was about ten of us out last night. As the whole regiment had been given the night off we thought we would go off to Lincoln instead of Scunthorpe; we ended up in the club by the bus station, The Light House I think it's called. Dinsdale and Britnal got themselves hammered and Geordie Gordon was looking out for them, I seen Geordie go out of the club about ten minutes before the rest of us. I hadn't seen Dinsdale or Britnal leave, so I think Geordie had gone out to look for them, when we all got out of the club, none of us could see them, so I went back into the club. I seen one of the doormen, and informed him I was looking for three of my mates. That was when I got a thought he knew something, as he told me not to worry, you will see them soon, they won't be away too long he said. At the time I didn't think too much about it, but now I think he knows what has happened."

B.S.M. Welsh had a look of concern on his face but cast it away quickly. "Let's not jump to conclusions, wait until this afternoon and see if they come back, if not we will start to look into what you have just said."

Wilson added, "Watt, you go to the gym, if Dinsdale comes in, let B.S.M. Welsh know straight away. If there is no sign of them by 12:00 hours I want you back up to see me."

Tony felt a little relief. "OK, yes Sir, will do."

Tony was dismissed and went down to the gym to start his work. When he got there, Glen had already started the lesson for him. There was one more P.T.I. working in the gym so Glen called him over to finish off. Glen could see Tony was not right. Tony had gone straight into the gym office, Glen followed. Tony sat down, Glen could see he was about to cry. Glen asked what had been said with the B.S.M.s. Tony explained it all to Glen, his eyes full of anger and worry. Glen was of the same mind as Tony, but had to keep Tony together, they knew Kenny wouldn't stay out if all was ok. He was the same as me, we both loved the army and the jobs we did and wouldn't jeopardise it for anything. Glen thought hard.

"Look Tony if we get nowhere with the B.S.M.s this afternoon, we will get the lads together and go down tonight and find out what has gone on. These are our lads, we've got to make sure they are ok."

Dunc and Donny were working in the hangar, sorting out the DM181s that had returned from the Falklands that morning. Dunc had felt guilty for not looking for us last night and Donny was of the same opinion. Bob Wilson called for them to his office.

"Sit down lads, I think we have a problem here, I don't know Geordie as well as you lads, but Brit I do know, he wouldn't go A.W.O.L. would he?"

"No Sir!" replied Dunc.

"Let me in on what is going down here."

Donny said, "There were eight of us that decided to go to Lincoln, we knew that the rest of the regiment would be heading to Scunthorpe, so we decided to stay away from trouble. We had been in one or two bars and decided to head to a club, I don't know the name of it—"

"That's ok, Tony has given me the name," Bob interrupted.

"I could see Kenny and Brit getting drunk, so me and Geordie had decided one of us should look after them. As he knew Kenny was not a big drinker but needed a good night, Geordie was not as drunk as me so we decided that it would be him, I seen Kenny and Brit head outside. Geordie decided he would follow them, he said if he could he would get a taxi with them, and head back to camp, that was the last time I had seen them. I wasn't concerned when Tony had said he couldn't find them, as I thought they had headed home."

"Right Dunc, did you see anything else that has made you doubt that?" Bob Wilson asked.

"Now that this has all happened Sir, I did see one of the doormen follow them outside, but as Geordie was following, I didn't think anything of it."

Wilson started to look a bit more concerned. He took a long look at Denis before he spoke.

"Right lads I will tell you what I think has happened. With what Tony has said and what you have just told me, I think the doormen have had a part in this. I think the doormen have given them a kicking and they will be in the hospital, we will check them out and in the meantime, I want you to speak with the rest of the lads that were with you last night, but get them to keep this between just the Lincoln lot. I don't want this getting back to the R.S.M Malaka. He will go off it and leave will be cancelled. And I don't want any of the lads sneaking out and causing trouble if we don't know with all certainty that the doormen had anything to do with it. Understood?"

"Yes Sir," they both said.

When Dunc and Donny came out of Wilson's office, Donny said that they will have to speak with Glen, Tony and Catton.

"Catton is A.W.O.L." Dunc said. "He headed off with that lass he picked up, and the BSM will not be interested in him as he gets out of the army in three weeks."

"OK, that will leave the four of us," said Donny.

They headed to the gym together in silence. Upon arrival Tony and Glen were there. All the lessons had finished for the morning so the gym was empty. Dunc pulled the doors closed and locked them up. Tony and Glen looked confused.

"Right lads," Donny said, "None of this leaves this room. We need your help."

8: Provisions

Back at the shed I was just starting to wake up, my eyes started to sting as they opened. A mixture of dry blood and sleep stuck to the lashes and the pain from the kicking I had was now starting to set in. Brit was sitting on the chair. He had moved it to the side of the mattresses to look over me and Kenny. I was not in a good shape, just like Brit and Kenny; my eye had swollen right up. Thanks to Brit. I looked over to where the stove was; Kenny was raking though it.

"What are you doing now mate?" I called out.

"There are some nails in the bottom of the fire, I am trying to get. They must have burnt some old pallets. If I can get them, we can use them as well."

"We need to get the stuff out of our pockets," I said. "If they decide to search us we will have the lot taken away."

Brit called out, "Get back on the mattress and lay down! I think they're coming."

Quickly I lay down and Kenny jumped on beside me. There was movement from the clinking chains holding the door then it started to open. It was a bright sunny day. The light shone through and like fire, burnt our eyes even more. Kenny sat up as though he had just woken with his hand shielding his eyes.

"Look lads," Steve said, "three sleeping beauties. It's the butler with breakfast!"

"I hope you have Alpen." Brit said. "That's the best cure for a hangover."

"Or you here to give us another kicking?" added Kenny.

"No, not this time." Steve chuckled. "Pete, just put the tray down on the old stove."

"Enjoy lads it may be your last one!" said 'the prat' Peter.

I was thinking of rushing him to make a run for it but just at the right time to stop me in my thoughts, Big Bob walked around the door. He was with four more men, one was Billy, the other three I hadn't seen before.

"Well, will this lot do you?" Big Bob said.

"Yes, I think they will be good for the new lads to the game," said one I didn't recognise. He was slightly smaller than Bob, and with lighter hair.

Brit called out, "Do you think you will get away with this? The Army will be looking for us!"

Bob's mate turned around and said,

"We have had more Army lads than you can think of and never been caught yet, so I don't think you will be any different. Big one A.W.O.L. as far as the Army is concerned, so why would they look for you anywhere but your home town? And that is not here, you *FUCKING COCKNEY CUNT*."

They all turned and left the shed sniggering and locked the door behind them.

Kenny rushed over to the stove to get the rest of the nails. As he did, he turned and said, "Look lads, we have sausage sandwiches and a pot of tea! Not bad of them is it?" No matter what the situation Kenny was always happy, and not even a kicking or the possibility of us not getting out of this alive could put his flame out.

Brit and I went over for the sandwiches and tea.

"I don't even care if they've had these sausages up their ass I'm still eating them," Brit said.

Our heads were banging from last night's booze and more probably from the multiple boots that had knocked with them. Food, *any* food was a welcome sight. After our cups and plates were bare we all started to think of ways to get out of this. Or what we could do if they did catch us out there. I shared my thoughts.

"We should wait until they let us go, and see what the situation is. We'd be fools to make a jump on them right outside. God knows how many men have joined up with these guys now."

Brit had been looking out of a crack in the door, where the lock was.

"Look lads, I can see a tree with three smaller ones around it, it has to be about four miles away. If we get split up we should make our way back to that point. What do you think?"

Kenny looked out with his good eye, I say his good eye, the better one of the two.

"You could be right mate, it is far enough away from here and if you look to the left of it, there is a valley so there should be water down there."

"What if they drive us away from here?" I said.

"Then we will have to think quickly for a different plan," said Kenny.

"OK, let us wait until it all starts and see, do you have all of the bits we collected?" I asked. They both nodded. "OK get them out of sight and don't let them find them."

We all started to put them down our trousers and in our socks and shoes. As we were doing that, we started to have another look around the shed for anything we could use. I looked up at the roof and in the rafters was a black bin bag.

"*Look!*" I called out. "What do you think could be in that?"

"Gold?" Brit called out.

"I hope so mate," said Kenny.

"Give me a bunk up mate and I will see."

Me and Brit held Kenny up while he grabbed it.

"Get me down I have a good grip on it. And it's heavy!"

We opened the bag and couldn't believe our eyes. It *was* gold to us; there was a small knife, snares, a pair of gloves and a water bottle. We had no idea why or how that stuff was up there but we took it as a good omen. But how would we get the bottle out of here? It was plastic so it should squash down flat without it splitting. It was nothing like an army standard issue, more of a soft drinks bottle. I stood on it squashing it flat. Kenny had a good look at it, it hadn't split. As he had a jacket on, he stuck it down one of the sleeves.

"Let's hope they don't find it," he said. "Let's put the bag back and hope they don't see it has been moved." We lifted Kenny back up and he placed the bag back to where he pulled it. I wondered who had put it there but like most things that I questioned lately I didn't expect an answer. We settled back down on the mattresses again.

I couldn't help but think our new finding was a bit too good to be true. How the hell would Big Bob and his goons have missed this? Maybe a trap? Maybe left by the last sorry troop that was held in this cage? Or maybe Billy? Well, who or whatever fortuned us with this gear I was grateful. Hope started to rise now our odds have been evened a little.

9: Recon

Back at camp Tony, Glen, Dunc, and Donny had decided to go back to the club that night to see what they could find out. They awaited word from B.S.M. Wilson if any of the hospitals or the police had seen us. By mid-afternoon they were getting impatient so decided to go to Wilson's office.

Upon their arrival the lads found Ian Tate was with Wilson and it didn't look good. Wilson opened the door to his office and beckoned them in. "In you go lads, we have things we need to discuss." His face didn't convince them that they had good news. "Me and Ian have been on to the hospitals and the police all day and no one has seen or heard from them." Wilson slowly gritted down on his teeth and glanced over to make sure his office door was closed. "So, we think you could be right Tony. The doorman knows something. What have you decided to do …?" He looked just at Tony, and Tony looked down the line at Glen, Dunc and Donny. Wilson brought Tony's attention back to him with a smile and added "… Because I *know* you all will have been thinking of something."

"Yes Sir," Glen said, "we have. And I think we should go back to the club and ask around."

Donny piped up, "Why don't you all go in together?" he said, looking at Glen, Tony and Dunc, "and I will hang around by the doormen, they aren't going to just tell you what has happened, and they didn't really notice me when

I was there." This was one of Donny's greatest skills, he noticed everything. He read body language very well and could always pick up on the things that were not said.

"You lads cause a bit of a scene, making it clear you're from the base and after you leave I will see what they have to say."

"OK, we'll go for that," said Dunc looking at the others. "But if we get nowhere, we go back and smash the place up!"

Ian broke his silence and looked to Wilson, "I think Donny is right." He then looked to Donny, "And no disrespect mate but you don't look like a soldier. But you *do* look like a doorman. If I put two of my lads that don't look like soldiers to keep an eye out in the club as well, we might just get somewhere."

Wilson's face looked lighter. "What do you think, lads?" he asked.

"Yes Sir, it might work," said Dunc. Donny looked happy that his plan had been accepted. Wilson took over with the finality of the plan.

"OK, so tonight we'll start light. Donny, Ian and Tony will go down. Dunc and Glen, you will stay away for now, I don't want it going wrong, because I know if they don't give us anything you will kick off and we will get nowhere."

"OK Sir," said Glen. "But if you don't get anywhere we can then go and kick the shit out of them."

Bob smiled as he told of the second part of the plan looking to Glen.

"Yes, if it will make you happy Sir," added Glen.

We all knew Glen liked a punch up and was good at it as well. Tony asked Glen if he would stay away so they could give it a go; he agreed under one condition.

"If you don't get what you need tonight I will be going down there tomorrow. And *no one* tries to stop me."

Glen was a joker, he loved to make others crack up but there were few times when he spoke without his trademark smile and you knew he meant business. They all nodded. They knew this could not be dragged out and knew that the team didn't get answers tonight they couldn't and wouldn't leave it another.

"OK lads that is fine," said Ian.

They left the office leaving Ian and Wilson. Ian stood up and flattened the creases on his shirt.

"We doing the right thing Bob?" he asked.

Wilson stood up and walked to the small window that was on the east wall. He looked at the regiment doing training exercises outside. They moved like a flock of birds, in unison. The stronger looking over the weaker. He noticed two officers from 7 battery, Sparks and Powell, a couple of jokers but they were good men. Sparks took Powell under his wing after he lost his two brothers during the Falklands war. He kept him going, kept his recklessness in line after his devastation took over. There was no greater display of spirit of the army. Officers may play rough and give each other discord and shit like it's on sale but we look after our brothers. No exceptions.

"We'll find our lads Ian and if those doormen had anything to do with it …" Wilson turned back to Ian,

"… *I'll nail them to the fucking wall myself.*"

10: 24 Hours

The light started to dim as dusk set in. We had been alone most of the day and the absence of any adrenaline pumping through our bodies had left Kenny, Brit and I feeling the true effects of the last two days.

Prat Peter had visited us twice with the supervision of Billy to drop in some food and water, but the rations were barely enough to fuel one grown man never mind the three of us. I suspected Peter would be doing this off his own back to even his chances if he came face to face with us when this 'hunt' began. Keeping us weak slowed our healing and if the lads felt as weak as I did then I questioned a million times in my head how three blind mice would prevail against Bob and his men. I tried to sleep but the silence was too deafening. We were agitated and restless and needed something to happen.

"I'm gonna take down Big Bob first, get the boys shitting their pants then I'm going for that little dick Peter, what a prick he is lads. Then I'm gonna save the last of my strength for Stevie dumb-fuck. Thinks he's a big man but he ain't seen little Kenny from Hartlepool fight properly yet!" Me and Brit burst out laughing. Poor Kenny didn't stand a chance in his current state and he knew this. His eyes were swollen so much he'd be lucky to spot the sun in the sky if he looked up but he kept positive. My face and ribs ached from laughing but it was worth it, just to lose myself for a moment. Pain meant I was alive, laughter meant I was still hopeful and having my two brothers with me meant I was not alone.

I had just started to drift off when I heard movement from outside. It was now pitch black but a car's headlights gave a gentle luminescence to the steel shed. I could just make out the faces of Kenny and Brit.

"Supper time you think lads, Chinese or maybe an Indian?" I tried to keep spirits up but I didn't think they cared for my sentiment. Quietly I said to Kenny, "If they come in don't wind them up mate, we might get another kicking and we can do without that. Just go along with whatever they say or do. This could be the best chance we have. You got away with gobbing off the last time but this time you may not be so lucky." Kenny agreed, but I knew the pocket rocket could only take so much and I dreaded to think of him getting another kicking to the face. That would be his endgame.

Brit edged closer to us. "Try and look as weak as you can boys, give them a false sense of security. They may give us a little more time to get healed up."

Just then the door opened.

Five men stood there, Big Bob, Steve, Billy and two more we hadn't seen before. As they walked in one of the new men looked down his wide flared nose,

"Two of them aren't very big, but that one looks good for me." As he looked over at me. Bob replied,

"The little ones are feisty and can take a kicking. They will give you some fun on the hunt." Bob turned to the two new men, "Go and check them out."

They walked towards Kenny and I thought we are going to have to start fighting now as Kenny won't be able to stop himself from retaliating.

He was sat on the mattress as one of them leant over him, "Where are you from little fella?"

Holy shit! My legs instantly flinched to stand to get to Kenny's aid as I knew he was going to make a jump at these two – one thing you did not do was call him 'little'. Kenny looked up at him, turned to Brit sitting next to him, then looked back at the man: "Let us go please! We haven't done anything! We won't tell anyone about this! Please let us go!"

I had to bite my lip to hold back the shocked face I would have undoubtably started to make. Brit, I could imagine, was doing the same.

The man looked at Big Bob and said, "That is what we like, someone who is crying for his mammy."

They turned and walked out the shed laughing. As they did so Pete came in with some food. He put a tray on the floor and said, "Make the most of it lads, you will only have one more feed before the game starts tomorrow night."

That was not good, we could see that it was dark outside so we had about twenty-four hours before it begins. We all got stuck in to the food, a hotpot I think and it was not bad. I turned to Kenny, "So you want your mammy, do you?"

Brit laughed and said, "Well done mate, that has got them on the back foot, as they now think you are an easy target. Or one to leave for the newer lads."

If we could have seen his eyes they would have rolled.

"That was the hardest thing I've EVER had to do lads. You tell anyone I begged to those fuckers and I'll lock yous in a cabin and hunt you down myself!"

We all laughed but I said, "Yes, I agree Kenny, but you will have to keep that up, *every* time they come in here."

He stopped eating for a moment as he realised I was

right. His momentum slowed for the rest of his meal until he was finished. "Look, I need you to do something for me Geordie," Kenny then asked.

"Yes, what is it mate?" I answered.

"Cut my eye open."

I nearly released my hotpot back to its bowl.

"*ARE YOU OFF YOUR FUCKING HEAD?* Why the fuck would I do that?" I knew Kenny wouldn't ask me anything like this if he wasn't sure. He was a bit of a hothead, but he wasn't stupid.

"It's a trick I was shown in the boxing gym. When your eye is as bad as mine you slit the swollen bit under the eye. Then the swelling goes down. I'll be able to open it, and I am going to need both eyes out there. Geordie, you have medic field training, I know it's not ideal but you can do it. The swelling will go right down and in about three hours it will be gone. If we are going to be hunted, I want to see all around me, so I have a chance."

Brit nodded. "He's right Geordie, it will work, I have seen the same at the boxing club I went to."

I was speechless, I knew what he was asking made sense but I couldn't deal with the guilt If I didn't do it right, but Kenny was dead if I didn't help him. My gut reacted before my brain could process and spoke for me,

"Well, if it works and you two know what you are talking about, Brit get on with it, because *I'm* not fucking going to do that!"

As soon as I said it I regretted it. I knew Brit would step up, but he hadn't the training I had. If anyone should, it should be me.

Brit immediately got the knife he had hidden on his

right leg. He took out his lighter, checked that the knife was sharp enough, and started to heat it with the lighter. Kenny put his head against the wall of the hut and twisted his jacket arm into a gag and bit on it. Brit took a tissue out of his pocket and moved close to Kenny. He paused till his hand was steady then cut the skin under the eye and pressed the tissue on it. I couldn't believe Kenny just sat and took it. The blood ran down his face and dripped onto his jumper. When they finished Kenny took the hanky and just held it over the cut, trying to nip it together. After a while Kenny moved to the mattress and lay down. The bleeding had stopped so keeping his head raised he rested it on his folded-up jacket.Brit set down soon after. After ten minutes I heard the heavy breathing of the lads deep in slumber.

But I was awake, the most awake I'd felt all day. *Welcome back adrenalin* I thought. The pain in my body had been replaced by numbness. I was in shock and ashamed. How could I have not helped Kenny when he needed me the most? I sat and paced most of the night, until the light started to replace the dark in our shed.

The last morning had dawned in our holding. I felt my guilt had reigned my thoughts too long, I had wasted vital time. I should have been making a plan, or any kind of strategy, that would help us through this next day. Maybe I should have spent time resting and building strength but instead I kept the rejection of helping Kenny spinning in my irritable head. If this was my last day it will have ended in another of my seemingly trademark failures.

I sat down on the floor and leaned on the mattresses where Brit and Kenny silently slept. My body was as exhausted as my mind and I slowly closed my eyes. Silence pulled its cover over my body ... I let go.

And then something hit me.

An idea that hadn't crossed my mind till this moment. It quietened everything else around me.

I had a *plan*.

11: The Lighthouse

Lincoln was a beautiful medieval town. Its historical buildings were quaint and charming. Its people were typical of the midlands, friendly and hospitable. A strong working-class spirit drove the wheels of its motor and kept its morals firmly buckled in.

Like most towns and cities as night falls all the friendlies seem to go underground. Locked in for the night while the other inhabitants emerge. They gathered together in the dimly lit streets and headed like moths to the bright lights of the bars and clubs. The lighthouse beacons and they come. This breed isn't like the light dwellers, they act as if the night disguises them. When the night comes they are invincible.

It was 21:00 and Donny, Tony, Wilson and Ian were waiting outside *Frankie's Bar* about 200 metres away from the club. They were soon joined by Evo, a Scouse lad, and Tommo from the midlands. These were the two lads Ian had offered to help infiltrate the club. He was right they didn't look like soldiers, but they were and good ones too. The plan had all been discussed at the base, they would go in the club in front of everyone else to keep look out and listen for any clues.

Donny walked in just in front of Wilson, Ian and Tony, who were dressed in uniform. He loitered for a few moments before moving to the cloakroom queue which was moving at a snail's pace as the young girl running the service struggled to take the coats, hand out tickets and chew her gum at the same time.

Ian approached the lad on the door; he was young, tall, more chubby than muscular and looked as if he was on work experience rather than a fully-fledged member of the doors patrol. His suit was baggy and looked like it was stolen from lost property. "Are you in charge here son?" Ian asked standing tall with his hands behind his back. "No, why do you ask mate?" questioned the lad. Wilson moved close to him, closer than comfort would usually allow.

"We would like to see the boss if you don't mind."

The lad ducked further into the doorway and shouted through to the struggling girl at the cloakroom who now stood before a mass of unhung coats with a handful of unorganised I.D. numbers. "Maddie, tell Ray I need him!"

Wilson and Ian stood at the door while Donny who needed to remain close to the doorway offered to help the highly-strung Maddie.

The head doorman appeared; he looked flustered and annoyed like he had been taken from something important. He was larger than the young lad on the main door, clean shaven, chin and forehead as shiny as his polished bald head.

"Can I help you gents? I'm a little short-staffed tonight."

Tony was stood behind them as Wilson had instructed.

"We hope so," said Wilson. "Eight of my lads came down here last night for a drink, and only four of them have returned, we were hoping you may have seen them?"

The doorman's eyes slid left, "No, sorry mate. We have hundreds come through the doors last night and we wouldn't be able to pinpoint any one." Ian asked if they had CCTV they could have a look through. The head doorman went red in the face and laughed. "We don't have anything like that here mate, sorry."

At that point, the young doorman moved further into the doorway, limiting his visibility while exhaling deeply. His eyes moved to Donny who was standing a few feet from him.

"What are you doing stood there pal? The club is in there!"

As Donny's coat had already been hung up and Maddie had caught up with her backlog he said, "I am waiting for your boss. Was just giving the lass here a hand, I am looking for work as a doorman." Quick thinking by Donny. He did look like a doorman, the right size and build.

"Just hang on a minute," the young doorman said.

Wilson knew his questions weren't getting him anywhere; he knew from the very first moment he stood at the doorway of the club.

"OK, thanks mate, but if you hear anything will you phone this number please." He handed him a card with the camp's number on it. The doorman nodded and stuffed it into his pocket with the likelihood of it never seeing the light of day again. Wilson, Ian and Tony walked off and the head doorman walked back inside the doorway rolling his eyes then sending a powerful glare to his colleague. The other said in a loud voice to try and drown out the tension, "This lad is looking for work, do you have any going for him boss?"

He turned to Donny and looked back to the fifty-strong queue waiting outside. "I think we might, come with me mate and we can have a chat."

Donny followed him into the club. The music was loud and the place stunk to high heaven of stale beer and cigarettes and desperation, something you never usually notice after a few drinks. He could see the two 9 battery lads sitting in the corner. He gave them a discreet nod and followed up a set of five steps and into an office.

"Take a seat mate," the head doorman said. Donny sat on the seat next to the desk, the doorman sat on the desk, looking over Donny's head as he began to speak before moving his attention to Donny's eyes.

"So mate, why do you want a job here?"

Donny was good at thinking on the spot, "I have just moved into the area from up north and don't have a job yet."

The Doorman edged further on the desk, it groaned as it took more of his weight, "Have you worked the doors before?"

"Yes, at *Nancy's Bar*, it is a club up in the lakes, I worked there for about a year and half before I had to move up to Newcastle for a new job."

"Did you work the doors in Newcastle?" he asked.

"No, my job was factory shift work, and I didn't get many weekends off to work back in the clubs."

The head doorman rubbed his temple and before he had a chance to fob Donny off he thought he best pipe up to sweeten the offer.

"Do you get many of them fucking squaddy pricks come to the club?"

He looked back at Donny's eyes, this time slightly bloodshot. "No, why do you ask?"

Donny flared his nostrils. "I don't like them. A bunch of them give one of my old friends a good kicking and put him in hospital for a long time. They all think they are gods, but you know they are just a bunch of daddy hating cunts that need the uniform to get a shag."

The doorman cracked a sideways smile.

"I try to keep away from them, or I might do something I might regret," Donny added.

The doorman lifted his brow, "Don't worry mate, we don't like them either. Well, if you are up for it, you can start tomorrow. I am two men short as they had to go away for three or four days so I really could use a lad to help my boy downstairs."

Donny couldn't believe he'd got in. Trying to hold back his pride, he quickly said, "Yes mate, that would be great, what time should I come along?"

"Get here for about six thirty, I can show you around and introduce you to the rest of the lads."

Donny stood up and shook his hand.

"Great, see you six-thirty." As he walked out the office, he was just going down the five steps when the head doorman called out, "My name is Ray and I might have a bit more than a job for you, but we will speak tomorrow about it."

"No problem Ray, I am Paul but I get Donny, see you tomorrow." Donny turned and headed back to the club's exit. He didn't want to look too interested in what he was on about, but he had a good idea it had something to do with Geordie, Britt and Kenny. Donny headed off through the club, he didn't look back at the two 9 battery lads in the club, he was too close to something. Head down, get out, don't blow this was what he kept repeating in his head.

He reached Maddie to get his coat. As she went through four coats that did not belong to him an older doorman, who looked like he had been brought out of his P.J.s and a date with the T.V. to help out, was talking to the younger one who first stood as he had come in.

"There were only three lads last night I heard, not four I am positive. I will check with the boss when he comes down later." Donny didn't look at either of the men, he concentrated on fastening his long-lost coat, head down, get out, don't blow this.

They had arranged to all arrive and leave in separate cars. No one to speak to each other until they returned to camp. Donny walked as casually as he could down the street. He kept his head straight and eyes forward. He reached the jeep parked in a back lane, five streets from the club. A few night dwellers still roamed the streets but they were mostly clear. He climbed in the jeep and sat a moment digesting what he had heard. Fitting the pieces together in his head.

His mind ran amok and before he knew the dashboard clock read 22:45. *"Fuck!"* Donny searched for the jeep keys, he He hadn't noticed he hadn't even started up the jeep yet.

The jeep started with a growl, alarming a few drunken youths a few feet in front. The journey back to base would take about 20 minutes, maybe 15 with no traffic. Donny knew he'd need the time to prep for asking the right questions tomorrow night. Subtle enough to go under the radar but specific enough to get the facts. The jeep let out another loud growl and tore away into the night.

Back at base it was 23:22 when Donny headed straight to Tony's room and, as he hoped, Tony was waiting for the lowdown.

"You *did it* Donny! You're *in!*" Tony shouted as he smacked his hands together. "We will go and see Wilson in the morning as planned! He'll have to let you have the day off tomorrow, so you can get your head down before going to work in the club." Donny nodded and headed out to his room but the inertia of his success kept him walking to Wilson's room. He didn't know how Wilson would react to his arrival at this late hour but he had to tell him their mission had been a success.

As he turned the corner to Wilson's room he saw he was sitting by the opened door. Wilson stood as he saw Donny. He nodded, "I was hoping you wouldn't wait till morning Donny. Tell me what you've got."

12: Surface

Tony woke, his sleep had been limited and his mind felt as fatigued as his body. Donny had made his first step to infiltrate the club and last night had given him a buzz that they were getting somewhere. Reality of the situation had kicked in when he tried to close his eyes and kept him far from sleep. The next steps would hopefully find the location to Geordie, Kenny and Brit and hopefully get them out of harm's way. Why they were taken, what they were going through and what state they'd be found in made it hard for Tony to settle in his soft, warm bed. He was usually up with two black coffees and an hour run under his belt but at 06:45 he lay motionless watching the shadows play on his ceiling. The morning parade would start soon, the lads would meet and any new information gathered by Ian's men would be shared.

He headed for the morning parade meeting Glen on the way. BSM Wilson was there waiting as normal. When the parade was over, Wilson asked them along with Dunc and Donny to go to his office and he would meet them there.

The last few days some of the lads on the parade knew something was going on, but what they hadn't worked out yet. Tony's mood had become more sombre, he hadn't been as playful as he normally was. He knew if they had the information they would all be there stood with them, probably in full gear with an unauthorised tank or two but at the moment this was a delicate matter and the fewer the better would help with this mission. It was 08:30 as Wilson walked into his office followed by Tony, Glen, Dunc and Donny waited inside, hands behind their backs, eyes fixed upon their boss.

"Sit down gents." Wilson started, "I have some disturbing news." He paused as if to allow the facts settle in his own mind first. "You will all know what Donny has done by now, signed up to be a doorman. He begins tonight so we need to assist him with anything he may need help with."

The lads looked at each other and nodded. They all knew Donny would already have an itinerary in his head. He was like that, his silence you never took as ignorance or stupidity. Donny took everything in, he liked to work thing out, work people out before he spoke or took action.

Wilson looked to his door, checking it was closed. "I've just finished speaking to Ian's men who joined us last night, Evo and Tommo. What they overheard does not leave this room. If we don't handle this carefully we risk putting Geordie, Kenny and Brit in further danger. They overheard a doorman talking about 'Going out with the wolves' as he called them. Something he is very excited about. They heard him say he would be leaving tonight at 01:00 hours from the club. He said they have three 'live-stock'. We assume this 'live-stock' is Geordie, Kenny and Brit. We know Catten went off with a lass last night, he's still A.W.O.L. but we don't think he is with them." He took a deep breath and stared down at his desk. "I've heard stories like this before, not often, but it's something I've heard majors telling new recruits when I've toured around the camps in the south. They used to warn of circuits working the clubs and pubs who would take the most drunken and wasted men they had, tie them up, beat them to a pulp and take them to the middle of nowhere and let them go…" He paused for a moment. "…to be *hunted*."

The four sat dumbfounded. They had put certain pieces together but hearing Wilson say it formally made each one feel sick. How can things like this happen?" Glen spat. Wilson looked at Glen, Tony, Dunc and Donny in turn.

"For money? Power? Hate? Who the fuck knows what goes though these sick bastards' minds but if we get lost trying to understand the minds of madmen, we will lose the opportunity we have before us."

Wilson was right. The most important thing right now was to get our men out and then deal with bringing these circuits down. Any police involvement now would slow everything down. They would have to conduct their own investigations taking time. The 'wolves' could get nervous and Geordie, Kenny and Brit would be long gone. Bodies buried in a shallow grave in a remote forest. They needed to do this themselves for now.

Wilson continued, "Donny, I want you to go to the club as you have agreed to start your shift."

Donny nodded, "Yes Sir, I am going for 18:30 hours."

Wilson went on, "Before you do, go to the Signals department and get fitted with a tracer device. You will be ok, it looks like a watch so they won't notice it. It is in case they ask you to go along to wherever our lads are. Glen and Dunc, I want you to go to the M.T. and sign out the Signals car, it is all rigged up with radios and a tracker locator; I have spoken to both departments so they will have them waiting for you all. Tony, you will come with me but I need you to get the second car from MT first. Glen, Dunc, you need to be in full combats and be ready for action. Donny and Tony, you have yours in a bag, ready to change if we need to. Donny, yours will stay with me and Tony. You all need to go down to the stores and sign out rations for five days and get enough for twelve men in total, just in case it drags on. Take your survival kit as well Glen, I know you have another special kit you take on exercise, take it with you."

Glen was a hunter, he had all kinds of kit for hunting and survival, so he would have anything we would need. Most not being of the army's 'standard issue'.

Wilson picked up the phone and rang Ian. "Bring them in," he said.

A few minutes passed and the office was silent, a welcome interruption arrived when Ian entered the office with two gunners Tony, Glen, Dunc and Donny didn't recognise. Dunc stood up and put the kettle on allowing Ian to take his seat. He poured three cups of black coffee. It wasn't a milk and sugar type of meeting he thought. He handed out the cups and stood behind Tony.

Ian looked at Bob. "I have given them the story Bob, the lads are willing to help." He looked to the new gunners. "Evo and Tommo did a good job last night lads and they will now assist us in the ops room but I've drafted two more seasoned men to help us with the rescue."

He introduced the two new lads Steve Platt and Jock Hughes, good lads and exemplary gunners. They both knew Geordie, Kenny and Brit making their interest stronger in the success of what happens next. Platt and Hughes were smaller than the others but very fit. They used to run circuits with Geordie and Kenny and had enjoyed learning martial arts with them. What's more they looked out for Geordie when he first joined up. They helped him after his rocky start and kept some of the bullies off his back.

Wilson reiterated the plan he had just given. Ian offered further support and took any further questions from Platt and Hughes. Ian was a good soldier, he had worked hard in his time in the army and rose to BSM after only a few years. He knew combat, he had seen action and had a sound strategic mind. Bob Wilson respected him and although it was seldom seen in front of their subordinates their friendship was always apparent.

"OK lads we'll meet back here at 16:00 hours to make sure we are all ready and go over the plan once more. Me and Bob will inform the R.S.M., just in case anything goes wrong he will give use the backup we might need."

Bob nodded, "OK gents, you are dismissed."

They had everything in place so decided to head to the cook house for a last chance meal. They took Steve Platt and Jock Hughes with them to run though everything and get to know their new teammates. After their meal it was all in place. Tony had picked up a tracker watch for everyone. This meant the car could track everyone's whereabouts and keep comms going, but most important Donny could be tracked. This was for two reasons, one, so they could track one of their teams and two if Donny got found out, they would be to get a location on him.

The men finished packing their equipment in silence, all running through all the strategies and possibilities the next twelve hours would hold. None knew the state they'd find the missing men in or if they'd find them at all. Uncertainty was the enemy but one thing all these men feared the most was that this is just the surface they were beginning to peel away. What if these hunts had been going on for years? What if so many of the A.W.O.L. soldiers over the years had suffered the same fate as Geordie, Kenny and Brit?

It could have been them and this terrified them more than anything else.

HELL'S HEROES

13: Purgatory

The hut door opened and three bowls of tomato soup were put on the floor. The deliverer we couldn't see as he had his face covered.

"Get that down you lads."

We didn't move at the gesture. We stayed where we were and waited for the door to close again. Prat Peter's voice came from the gap between the doors,

"LAST SUPPER BOYS!" he shrieked. This was the third last super we have had. I thought that they were trying to keep us restless, frustrated and on edge by keeping the threat level up to fuck with our heads.

"I think 'the prat' is right this time lads. This is probably the last one," said Brit.

"You could be right mate," I said.

The shadow in the gap doorway shifted. Prat Peter was watching us. Taking in any fear or nerves he could absorb from us. We gave him none.

"The fun will start tonight so eat up," Pratt said through the gap. Turning his eye back into us. He started to laugh, "You had better be good runners."

Still we gave him no reaction, we simply gulped down the lukewarm soup and old dry bread. Bored from no reaction we heard his footsteps taking him away from the shed and most likely back up the arsehole of Big Bob.

Brit spoke first.

– 69 –

"I think we must be getting a head start on them."

"Yes, that's what it sounds like," Kenny replied.

"Don't get too excited," I said. "I don't think they will let us have too much of an advantage, do you? I think it will be tonight they get us out. This is the third last super we have had, I think they are trying to keep us from resting. It will be as dusk sets in. We don't know the lay of this land, they do so we have the last of today to get ready."

I put down my bowl and looked though the gap in the door once more to check on the RV point we had agreed on. I felt apprehensive telling Kenny and Brit of the plan I had thought of. I hadn't brought up my guilt of not helping with Kenny's eye and hoped the lads hadn't been stewing over it the same as I had. I needed to stop being a pussy, the time was now, we needed this time to go through it and think of any variables. Before my brain was even ready my mouth already began to speak: "Kenny, you need to go on your own."

Kenny paused with his soup. "What are you talking about Geordie?"

My face began to flush. "Sorry mate, I'm a little ahead of myself. I have an idea. You are the fastest and now the swelling on your eye has gone down you will have a better chance on your own as you will probably take two of them out with no problem." I wasn't making sense and I knew it. Kenny and Brit looked confused and their stares were starting to burn my skin.

"Slow down John, what are you talking about?" Brit said calmly.

I took a breath, Brit never called me 'John'. It was a shock hearing him speak to me like my mother would but I knew it was more out of serious concern. Maybe it was the stress and guilt of the last day affecting me more than I'd care to admit but I needed to keep my shit together. One more deep breath, a long blink and I sat back down with the lads.

"OK, let me tell you a plan I've had. We don't know where we are. How close the nearest roads are and if we take a chance to get out of here on foot I don't think we'll make it. I think we need a car. When we get out we run a mile or so out then Kenny, I think you should split off and head to the rendezvous point and wait there till this area has cleared out. Me and Brit will keep them distracted away from you. Still, when it's dark you head back here and get one of the cars ready for us. You're faster than me and Brit and you'll be able to take out any men that have stayed to babysit the camp here. Slash the rest of the tyres so none of the other fuckers can get away. If me and Brit can get back here as well we will, but if not we'll keep them at bay while you get away and bring back help."

Kenny and Brit looked to the ground assessing the plan.

"You guys are fast too," said Kenny.

"Yes, but you can run fast and long distances. If you get away we can try to hold them off your tail, this way we might get one away and get help back," said Brit.

Kenny thought a moment, he knew he was faster and with his boxing training he could take care of himself. "OK you win, I will do it," he said.

Brit piped up with his sarcasm, "He will only win if I look after him." He followed this with a wink. Kenny had a good laugh, "Well I think I have the easy job getting away, but you Brit I feel sorry for, having to put up with Geordie longer than I have to." They both had a good laugh, this was good, as it meant they both had started to feel better, although we are still in pain with the bruising, we can fight through it.

We got stuck into the soup. After Brit finished his he got up and started to have a last look around to see if there was anything else we could take with us. I checked Kenny and Brit to see if all items had been hidden well out of sight and as discreet as possible in case we were frisked.

We sat down on the mould stained piss covered mattresses and started to go through the plan. Time was starting to pass and we all started to get a bit uptight. Kenny was up and down, looking though the gap in the door. Nothing was going on outside, no movement, just lights from the hut next door. Kenny got us up off the mattresses and started to get us exercising. "We need to start and try to get through the pain we are in lads and limber up," Kenny said. We knew he was right and would be sorry if we didn't when we set off. If they planned to give us a kicking before they start we needed to be ready for it and warming up our muscles would lessen the blow. Kenny's eye had gone right down, he could see OK out of it now and he had started to feel better all round.

The exercise was just a light workout, but it felt like hell, it was agonising. Brit started to laugh at Kenny. "Look at his face Geordie." He was scrunching it up like an old prune, and with the state of his eyes, we couldn't stop laughing but trying to keep the noise down and hold the pain in our ribs back at the same time. Kenny called us to stop.

"We upsetting you Kenny?" chuckled Brit.

"Shut up and listen!" Kenny snapped back.

Outside we could hear a car coming down the track. We went closer to the door to see if we could see anything. There were two cars coming slowly down the track. This must be the rest of the wankers coming to have us I thought. Just then Steve came out of the hut next door and looked down to the cars. He shouted back into the hut saying it was the lads from London.

"They have made it, fuck me!" Brit called out.

"What's wrong mate?" I asked.

"If it's the twats from the West End we will have our work cut out. They are cunts!" said Brit.

Kenny laughed, "You should see the ones from Hartlepool! They'd hang you!" Me and Kenny just looked at each other and laughed. Brit didn't get the joke, but to be fair this was not the time to be joking around. This was going to be one of the hardest things we would have to go though in our lives.

The cars pulled up and seven big men got out, they all started shaking hands and hugging.

"Good to see you all again lads," Big Bob said. "Come in and we can go through the plan," he said as they headed back to the hut."

"Steve, get the kettle on for the lads!" one of the new ones called out. He was obviously one that had been on a hunt with them before. They all went into the hut and we could no longer hear words only the rumble of talk and laughter. We looked at each other.

"This is no joke lads," I said. The look on all of our faces had changed. For the first time, we all had the same thoughts. This was going to be life or death. We couldn't get out of it, it was going to happen, we had no say in it. All we could do was wait for the last hour. The final hour.

Dusk had set in.

Suddenly shit got very real.

14: A Day in the Life

It was 16:00 hours. Donny, Tony, Dunc, Glen had arrived at B.S.M. Bob Wilson's office with Ian, Platty and Jock. They ran through the plan again and checked all the equipment was in good working order.

At 18:00 Wilson, Tony and Donny went in one car to the club. They dropped Donny at the bus stop about a mile from the club so they wouldn't be seen together. Wilson and Tony arriving at the club at about 18:30 hoping to speak with the head doorman one last time. The other four set off in the second car, leaving Ian behind to man the phones; they waited about three miles outside of town at the edge of a wood.

Wilson and Tony got nothing, the same lads on the door from the night before gave nothing away. Just as they started to leave Donny got off the bus just over the road from the club. The timing couldn't have been better. As Donny walked toward the club doors, the young, chubby doorman shouted, "Hi Paul!" as he approached. The older of the doormen looked on; the younger doorman said, "Hi, I'm Richie, Ray told us you were coming on tonight." Just then Ray emerged from the inner doors.

"Hiya mate," Ray said. Then looking at the older doorman, "This is the new lad that I told you about." The older doorman glared at Donny from head to toe, not saying a word and displaying an obvious note of threat that Donny would take a bit of Ray's favour away from him.

"Nice to meet you gents," said Donny. Using the opportunity of seeing Wilson and Tony outside he jumped straight into watering the seed he had planted on his first visit to the club.

"Those army pricks back again?" Donny asked.

"Aye mate, what a bunch of tossers!" Ray said, "Come with me mate and I will get you a jacket and badge, we all have to have the same clothing," he explained. "And you'll need an ID badge." As they headed to the office, Ray said, "You really don't like army lads do you?"

Donny immediately widened his eyes, "Nah not at all."

"Why was that again?" Ray asked.

"Some of them give one of my mates a good kicking to show off." Donny thought this was to see if he was giving the same story as last night.

"That's right," Ray said. "If you had the chance to get any of them back for your mate, would you?"

"Like a shot!" Donny replied.

They continued up the stairs to the office.

Hanging on the back of the door was a doorman's thick black coat.

"Chuck that on, Paul," Ray said while he pulled a blank ID tag out of his drawer. "And fill this in for me Paul, while I get you logged in."

Donny filled in the tag the best he could in the dim light of the office.

"So, is cash in hand alright for you mate? We don't have any fancy systems in place you might be used to. The bar manager just lifts our wages from his till for us," said Ray.

"That's great, yeah," said Donny, not expecting anything

less from this grotty club. He fastened up his coat, it smelled like old sweat and cheap aftershave. Ray clipped on the club's piss poor excuse for an ID badge on the coat while Donny put his hands in the pockets. He felt a used tissue, a lighter and some kind of business card. His attention was brought back to Ray when he spoke.

"Before we get started can I ask what are you doing for the next three or four days mate?"

"Not a lot. I haven't found work yet," replied Donny.

"Smashing, I might have something you'll be interested in. Don't mention it to Cooper, the old fart on the front, he'll take the huff with me as he thinks he's going, but something tells me you're better suited. Would you be up for coming with me somewhere, when we are finished tonight?" Ray said smugly.

Donny didn't want to sound overly keen, but he'd thought a lot about how to direct his responses to get the info he wanted. "If it's for a shag back at your house, I'm married Ray, you may wanna ask Cooper."

Ray laughed out loud and Donny joined in to win over the most merit he could. "Nah, nah, nothing like that!" Ray snorted out, "But believe me, you will have some fun!"

Donny felt it right to try and push a little more. It was less than ten minutes into his infiltration, no relationship or boundaries had been built up yet but Donny felt the moment arise. One thing he could always count on in all his observations of men who thought they were 'machos' is when you question their orientation, they feel the need to over compensate on their explanations. As if to explain themselves in the greatest level of detail, to banish the question from your mind. He looked straight down the barrel and played this to Ray. "So if you're not after a shag then what is it?"

Ray cleared his throat, "Have you heard of 'The *Hunt*?'"

Fucking bingo! thought Donny.

It was 21:00. Tony and Wilson waited in the car within eyeshot of the club as planned. If Donny was in trouble they would be there for his aid. The air was warm but the windows stayed up so their conversations could not be heard. They systematically checked the car phone. A relatively new piece of kit which resembled an office handset but with buttons on its reverse. Soon to be fitted in all high- ranking cars before a complete roll out over the year. Their minds were focused on what Donny was going through, playing out how he would handle each situation. Both knew he was the best choice for the job. He had a good understanding of how to work people and when to keep his mouth shut. His only flaw would be his attachment to Geordie, Kenny and Brit. Whether he could keep his head if he found the men who had taken them or hurt them. Just then the phone began to ring. The number brought up none of the caller I.D.s stored in its memory. Tony answered.

"It's Donny, I'm in."

Tony asked immediately, "Are you safe? Can you talk?"

"Yes, I'm at the phone box across the road from the club. I can see your car. I told them I'm ringing my wife."

Wilson motioned to Tony to take the phone.

"Donny it's Wilson, tell me what's happening."

Donny stood in the phone box looking toward the club, Cooper stood staring at him, too far away to hear or lip read but Donny knew he'd have to put on a show of marital dispute.

"I can't be too long so please remember all of this. Excuse my tone Sir, I'm gonna pretend to argue with you. The hunt starts at 03:00 hours, they have our lads held at least one and a half hours outside of Lincoln as we leave at 01:00 to reach their location. We do not know the location exactly, It only gets revealed on route by the driver that picks us up. It's planned to last up to four days. Do you have location on my tracker?"

Wilson looked to Tony, who got on his radio, Donny overheard Tony respond over the radio, "Yes, we have him, Sir."

"Great, I heard that, Sir." Donny continued. "Ray is the head doorman here at the club. His isn't usually included in the hunt as it's invite only but because our lads were caught here they have extended the invitation to him. The two other doormen here are too soft to compete with him so he's recruited me. He had doormen from Leeds helping him out when our lads were taken as he's really short staffed. I'm guessing it was them who took them away. *STUPID BITCH!! WILL YOU LISTEN TO ME!!*" Donny gestured wildly and banged his hand off the booth's window. "Sorry for that, Sir, just putting on a show. It's £500 per competitor, Ray is advancing me wages for my cut as he must be desperate to have a shot at this. There is a cash prize of 10 grand for the winning team so there must be at least 20 men plus to make it profitable for the organiser—"

"My god," Wilson interrupted. "This is big, I think we may indeed need help from the R.S.M. I'll contact him and get him to get a team ready."

"We should be prepared for a lot more men than originally thought but these men are not skilled like us," Donny continued. "If Ray is anything to go by, these men are stupid, Sir, it's more about the money and the title for bragging rights. As I can't give you an exact location and most likely won't get the chance to get to the phone again as it may raise suspicion, you will have to tail us at unnoticeable distance. We will be joined here by more men, maybe another five cars, so allow us to get well underway before you pursue."

"We understand Donny. You've done exceptionally. We are gonna get our lads back because of this. Keep your head cool and go as long with as much as you can."

There was a moment of silence.

"Thank you, Sir, I better go, I will see you all at the end of this." Donny returned the handset and let out a dramatic series of exhales for Cooper's benefit, and headed back over to the club.

"Trouble in paradise?" asked Cooper.

"You know what women are like," replied Donny.

"Never married myself," said Cooper.

I'm not at all surprised, you creepy little troll, thought Donny. "Really? I envy you," he said.

He worked the doors another few hours with Richie and Cooper, not much trouble for his first night. Ray remained out of sight. Maybe getting ready for his big shot tonight, calling everyone he knew to brag or maybe actually doing legitimate work. It was 23:35 before he was spotted at the front of the club shaking hands with some men. All dressed in the same thick black coats. Here we go, thought Donny.

One of the men headed to the front door while the rest followed Ray around the back of the club.

"Hello mate, I'm Mick." He gestured his hand to Donny.

Donny accepted it. "Donny, nice to meet you."

Mick held on to the shake a little longer than expected. "I've met you before, haven't I? I recognise your face." He spoke a little quieter guiding Donny a little further back into the club's doorway.

"I've not been in Lincoln long. I used to do the doors in the Lakes, maybe you've seen me there?"

"Maybe … anyway, Ray tells me you're his partner in the fun tonight," he said with a smile on his face.

"Yeah, not something I was expecting for my first night here but I'm well up for it," said Donny.

"It didn't look like your wife was as keen," chuckled Mick.

FUCK! thought Donny, how did he know that? He hadn't noticed anyone else around when he had called Wilson. He thought of a quick response. "Shit, has she been in mouthing off? I only said I was going off to do some training at other clubs."

"Nah, I saw you on the phone having your quarrel. I was parked just next to you."

Donny could feel his neck get hot and prayed his face didn't let on his discomfort. There had been a car with blacked out windows parked up a few metres from the phone box but it had been there hours. He had assumed it was Ray's and was most likely unoccupied.

"I hope I didn't embarrass myself. You know how women are when you say you're leaving them for a few days right?"

"Sure," said Mick. "Let's hope she doesn't spoil it for you. You know, letting her mouth go. They penalise you if anyone finds out about what goes on with the hunt. I mean, they *literally* cut off your penis." Mick said this with a completely straight face. Then burst out laughing. "I'm messing with you mate. You'll be cool. So, did Ray tell you what to expect?"

Donny was at a loss with Mick, he usually could read people quite quick, pick up on their mannerisms but Mick had thrown him. He couldn't yet tell if he was being played or if indeed Mick was just having a little fun with him. Donny had little option but to go along with Mick for the time being and keep up his act.

"Just the basics so far, he's been busy tonight. Maybe you can fill me in?"

"Of course," said Mick, edging Donny further away from Cooper and Richie's earshot. "I have worked the doors for years, up and down the coast. I was the one that got Ray the contacts from the clubs from down south."

"So there are more than just us going on the hunt?" asked Donny, keeping up the ignorant act.

"Yeah, we had 28 last count, mind there could be more now as some wait to see who's taking part before they commit. Some packs are stronger than others. If the big boys take part some of the weaker lads don't bother." Mick was so excited about the hunt, he couldn't stop himself from talking, probably giving away a little more than he should. "We normally split into teams of at least four, or thereabouts, and give the runners a thirty-minute head start. To start off with we will give the runners a hard time, knock them about a little and have a laugh with them. What happens at the end with the runners? You will have to wait and see … if you are lucky enough to be the catching group."

Donny needed more; anything else he could get to the lads at base could make a big difference.

"Where do you do it? Must be pretty remote if it's on three to four days."

"You aren't meant to know yet but we'll be leaving in a

few hours so I can't see the harm. It's out in the dales, we call it 'The Swamp'. It makes getting around out there pretty tough and stops the runners straying too far. You still up for it?" Mick asked.

"Dead right I am, I was told that they are army lads," said Donny.

"That's right, I think they come from the camp in Kirton Lindsey, I was here the night they were caught."

That confirmed to Donny, it had to be Geordie, Brit and Kenny. But Mick had been here on the night they had all been out, Donny hadn't noticed him with the doormen, he must have been out of uniform. He couldn't dwell on that right now. Hopefully Mick wouldn't spend too much time thinking it over. But if he was discovered he had to get the location, regardless of how vague, in case he was kept here.

But Mick was called off by Ray so Donny got back on the front door. He had to get the information back to camp.

Another thirty minutes passed before Richie shouted over "Donny, get yourself on a break, twenty minutes mate, but don't go far and keep your radio on – we may need you."

"Great, thanks Richie, where do I go for a cuppa?" Donny replied, he needed to get to a phone, but knew he couldn't go to the one in front of the club, in case suspicion arose.

"Head up to Ray's office but turn left instead."

Donny walked back into the club and headed toward the office. He'd try Ray's office for a phone. As he got up the steps Ray opened the door from the inside, Donny stepped back.

"You after something mate?" Ray said.

"Ah no mate, I was told to go on a break and was hoping to have a cuppa?" Donny said.

Ray motioned to the door opposite his office. "Yes that's fine mate, go up the stairs through that door, turn left at the top and there is a rest room we use, all you will need is there."

Donny smiled, "Cheers mate" and off he went.

When he got to the rest room, there were two other bar staff in already.

"Hi, I'm Donny, I have just started tonight. Is it ok if I make a cuppa?"

"Help yourself" one of them replied not looking up from a newspaper probably from before the Falklands. It was as much as they spoke to him. Donny started to make a cuppa and noticed at the end of the bench was a phone. If only he could get the chance to use it.

After ten minutes both lads drank their tea and left. This was Donny's chance. It was probably his last to use a phone so he went for it. As long as he got the new information to Wilson he could pretend he was calling his wife if anyone came in. He reached into his trouser pocket for the piece of paper with the car phone number on it. It wasn't there.

"Fuck!" muttered Donny, he'd left it in the phone box outside. He searched the jacket pocket in case he'd slipped it in there by accident. The tissue, lighter and piece of card the size of a bank card. He took it out. It was Bob Wilson's office card at base, this was the same coat Ray had on the night before.

"Thank you, Bob" he muttered. Donny dialled the number while looking toward the window of the staff room. It rang five times before changing ringing tone, it was probably on call divert as Wilson was off base. Great! he thought. A voice came from the other end,

"Hello, twelve Regiment duty clerk speaking, how can I help you?"

"This is Paul Donahue, is Bob Wilson or Ian Tate available?" Donny asked urgently.

"No, they are off base. Who are you again?" asked the clerk. Not many knew Donny's full name.

"It's Donny from Five Eight battery."

"Oh! Hi mate! It is Pipes, what are you doing ringing B.S.M. at this time? Tate isn't even in your battery, what do you want him for?" Donny didn't have time for this, in a quiet but stern voce he said,

"Pipes, don't speak just listen. Get a message to him A.S.A.P. and don't fuck about, do not say a word to anyone but Wilson or Tate and don't stop trying to reach them."

Footsteps and chatter could be heard from along the short corridor to the break room. Donny spoke low,

"It is happening on the Yorkshire moors, at a place called the Swamp, have you got that Pipes? Repeat it back to me while you write it down." Just then Ray and Mick opened the door to the break room. And stood staring down at Donny. He held up one finger and made a chatting motion with his left hand as Pipes repeated the correct information back to him from base. Donny lifted the tone in his voice,

"Yes sweetheart that's right. I'm sorry I shouted at you but I'm doing this for us. Now get some sleep, I love you. Goodnight." And then he hung up.

"Sorry lads, just thought I'd ring the missus and make a bit of peace or my life would be over when I got back." Ray smiled, while Mick looked out through the window down the corridor. Something was up, Donny thought this was it, he was caught and now he'd be the fourth lad to be beaten up and thrown in to be hunted. Under the table he clenched his right fist and with his left he got a good grip of his scalding cup of tea.

"Everything alright?" he asked.

"Sorry mate," said Ray, "Mick has been spotted by a crazy slapper he scored with the last time he was here and she's after him." Ray laughed. "He's hiding in here from her!"

Donny laughed and carried on drinking his tea. Releasing his fist. He looked down at the table and noticed he'd left out Wilson's card. It was too far to make a grab for discreetly. Donny looked up and saw Ray's eyes looking down at the card.

"Say Donny, have you been a naughty boy?"

15: The Pursuit

B.S.M. Ian Tate got out of the shower and started to get in his field squad gear. He hadn't thought he'd be letting his tools see the light of day so soon after the Falklands; ready for the next few days. He didn't feel any better and spent the whole three and a half minutes in the shower checking his radio.

He fastened his belt and picked up his bag when he heard someone running up the hall. He stepped out his door and bumped full force into Gary Pipes.

"What the hell Pipes!" shouted Ian.

"I'm sorry, Sir!" Pipes spluttered out of breath. "I've just spoke to Donahue, err Donny, Sir!"

"Donny has just called base?" asked Ian.

"Yes, Sir. Only a few minutes ago, Sir. He gave me a message." Pipes paused and looked down at his note he crudely made on the front of his Playboy magazine. Ian snatched it from his hands.

Yorkshire moors, the Swamp

"Did he say anything else?" asked Ian.

"No, Sir, just to tell no one but you or Bob Wilson err B.S.M. Wilson, Sir."

"Get back to your desk, call me at OPS 1 if you hear anything else!" Ian then sprinted toward the ops room where the rest of the team would be gathering, leaving Pipes on the floor. He did not stop.

When Ian entered he saw R.S.M. Richard Malaka was going over some of the plans with the lads he had drafted in; Ian ran to the cabinet at the end of the centre desk. He pulled out the large stack of maps that sat tidily inside and tossed them across the floor till he found the one he wanted. He unfolded the neatly folded map of the Yorkshire moors.

"Everyone over here!" he called out. Laying the map out across the tables he pulled out a pencil he kept in his left pocket. "Our men are here." Ian circled a large area of land on the map." It's a place locals call 'The Swamp'. I have been there before. It's a hell hole. It will take about seven hours at least for the lads to get out if they are in top form and they know where they are going, but I don't think they will, so I am sending out the backup team. They will be in four teams of four, I will give you the grid references of the four teams, as I am sending them to four separate locations." Ian wiped the heavy sweat that had gathered on his forehead. He wrote down the grid references and handed them to one of the lads. "Get these to Dunc and tell him to stand by for further instructions."

The R.S.M. held up his hands toward Ian's chest. Before he could say a word, Ian said "Donny has just called the base." Without another word R.S.M. Malaka got on the radio to Dunc while Ian moved the backup team into the room next door, so they were ready to go at a moment's notice.

Ian then contacted Tony and Wilson in the second car, team two as they now called it. Then went to OPS 2 to brief his four teams. They checked over their equipment for the last time and within 15 minutes were sent off.

The teams all got into the back of a four-tonner truck and would be dropped about five miles from their locations.

The truck was then to head to a small farm that was about ten miles north of the moors. The driver was to stay there until he was called for; the driver was Ian's younger brother, Robert Tate. He was well up on the area as he was the regiment's driving instructor and would take the lads all over to as many different terrains when teaching drivers.

Dunc was briefing his team on their instructions; they had all been sitting in a small wood at the side of the road. Glen got up as Dunc had finished giving out instructions and got into the car and started it up. Platty got up and headed for the passenger's seat, to act as navigator. Dunc and Jock got in the back. Jock had them all sync up watches with Glen's, he then got on to the radio and put out an all station call to sync; one by one they came back set ready. Jock called out 22:00 hours then called out, "Set, set, set!" Again, each team came back one by one: "22:00 hours set."

Wilson and Tony had got set at their location, as they still had to follow the car Donny would be in. Midnight came and Ian put out an all station call to check that all radios were still working. And that none of the teams had nodded off.

At 00:30 team two arrived at their location. Platty looked over the map, and informed the teams if this is the location where the swamp is Kenny, Geordie and Brit are going to find it hard work.

"If they get set free in the centre of this, it will take them about 15 to 20 hours to get to any of the roads around the moors and that is only if they set off in the right direction!" He looked again at the map and assessed the area around him. "It's reasonable to assume they will have to be in the centre of that area over there," pointing to his left. Platty got Dunc to contact Ian and confirm they are in the right location and if so they need to head further into the moors so it will cut down the intercept time.

"Any stronger chance of helping the lads, take it."

Ian confirmed. and agreed with what Platty had said. Ian then called all teams except Wilson and Tony to inform them to head to a new grid on foot and report back on arrival.

Dunc and his team put their car in a wood nearby, covered it in branches and wrote down the grid reference on their map. They set off with Platty who was still map reading. This was the best plan, as 'Platty' the lads would say, 'was shit hot with a map and compass.'

Donny got back to work at the front of the club. He tightened up and started to stop people coming in until they produced I.D. Mick asked what he was doing,

"Checking they are old enough to come in, right?"

"No mate, we don't do that here, if they have the money to pay, then let the fuckers in."

Donny sensed a level of discontent from Mick since the run-in at the break room. Donny thought he was done when Ray spotted Bob Wilson's card on the table. But Donny had managed another bit of luck with his quick thinking. He had told Ray that he'd just found it in the pocket of the coat he was wearing, along with the lighter but that, he joked, he was keeping. Ray seemed to accept this as he knew Donny was wearing his old coat and he himself had put Wilson's card in the pocket the night before.

It was 00:20 and Donny was starting to get clubgoers to leave; the time was getting on, and the club closed at 00:30 on a week night. He could feel the excitement from Ray and Mick as they crudely booted as many of the clubgoers out as forcibly as possible. They were joined in the process by the other doormen that had arrived earlier who no doubt had had a free night of drinks and girls while they waited for the club to close. They kept checking their watches and saying to one another "Not long now!".

Mick thought it would be good to have side bets,

"Ten quid each lads, and name the one you think who will get it first!" Steve piped up and said,

"Here is my tenner and I will get the big one. The Geordie!"

They all started to laugh and put their notes in. All picking a different lad as a target. Ray looked at Donny,

"Aren't you having a go mate?"

He found it really hard to blend in with them when they talked about his friends like a slab of meat. He warily smiled,

"No mate, I will just be happy to be there when one of them is caught. That's worth more than a few quid for me."

"Fair enough," said Ray, "just remember ten grand prize money if our team nails them. Imagine ya' wife's face when you go home with a few grand for her!"

The club was now empty and Donny was ready to go. The cars pulled up at the front of the club and Donny was told to get in the back one with three of the other doormen. One asked Donny if he was ready for it.

"Yes, no problems with me, mate," Donny replied. "Just show me the rabbit and I will catch it."

They all started to have a bit of a giggle.

"Not before us, you are the new boy mate!" one said.

The cars moved off. Donny asked how many was on the hunt, as he hadn't asked these men any questions yet.

"The last we heard from Big Bob there are twenty in total." One said, "Eight dropped out when they heard the cockneys were going. Those guys are *lethal!* You drop out though you still have to pay your fee so the prize money stays the same," said another.

"House always wins right?" said Donny.

"Big Bob always wins," two of them said together.

"We are meeting the rest at start line. There is a couple of sheds there, we will have a bite to eat and a cup of tea, meet the other lads and have a quick nap. We'll sort out what size teams we will have and sort out who will be with who," the driver said.

There were two cars and eight lads it total. They left the city centre, soon into the darkness of the countryside. The car was buzzing with chat and laughter. Donny was sitting behind the driver. He kept looking straight ahead, he was hoping Pipes had got his message out. That the lads were waiting at the moors, already set up and that Tony and Bob Wilson would be hot on their pursuit.

16: Tides

Ian sat in OPS 1 staring at the computer monitor. It was a large windowless room, that seemed the size of a football pitch when it was independently manned. The occasional small semi-cool gust of breeze from the desk fan was the only thing that took his attention. The room was hot and as a centre for operations at the base it was no surprise that many of the seniors referred to it as "The Pressure Cooker."

He rose from the leather swivel chair, leaving a heavy patch of sweat his ass couldn't bear to spend another moment with, and paced the floor in front of the monitor. Donny would be leaving the club soon and Ian had to relay every twist and turn to the rest of the team.

The computer terminal was an old model, refitted more times than Ian would like to guess, but it operated for the sole purpose of the global positioning system. The tech developed by the American military hadn't been at the base for long. Navstar developers had charged the military a small fortune for its use, Ian could not have thought of a better reason for it, this night. Its accuracy would locate Donny's position within a 1/4 mile radius as long as there was no heavy interference from land mass or cloud cover.

As his impatience grew, Ian chased the possibilities of Donny's fate from his mind. He was ready to get in a jeep and head to the moors himself if the G.P.S didn't reveal any signals. He pulled his hand slowly down his face wiping away the tide of fresh perspiration the pressure cooker had given it. As his eyes adjusted back to their surroundings, the monitor display had changed; the crudely animated map in black and electric green colours began to glitch and reposition. This was it. Donny was on the move.

Tony and Bob Wilson waited on the very end of the street of the club on the opposite end of the road which would lead them toward the motorway. The street was still very much alive since the club closed and there were enough taxis and drunken locals in the street to take attention away from their vehicle. Tony held his binoculars fixed on the row of cars parked outside the club. He hadn't seen anyone enter or leave them and was unsure if these cars were going to be used to take the doormen on their journey. He and Wilson never said a word. They kept the senses high and mind wound tight. Ian's voice startled both men,

"Donny is away, north to north west, if you head to the M62, I will keep you updated if there is any change."

Without a word Bob started the car. Ian's voice continued. He would call the rest of the team to inform them that the target was on the move. All four field teams replied informing him that they were in position and ready to move. The teams knew it would still be two to three hours before they would be required; one member of each team took it in turn to have a bit shut eye.

Dunc had Platty on first watch, Platty took the time to look over the map and noticed that in the east side of the moors there was two small buildings. At first, he thought they were farm buildings but then realised the land around them was all moor and there was no other house for miles.

He gave Dunc a kick. "Take a look at this Dunc, the two buildings over there, there is nothing around, that would suggest they are farm buildings, so I think that could be where the lads are being held."

Dunc checked it out and then give Glen and Jock a kick. They all had the same opinion. That had to be the place.

Platty contacted Ian and put it to him, Ian checked over his map and agreed, Dunc with the rest of his team decided to head in that direction. This would give them a great advantage if it was the right area but if not, it could be a big setback. It was a risk they felt they had to take.

Time passed and the doormen had stopped for a piss brake, Wilson and Tony were about ten minutes behind them. They also had to pull over. Ian had suggested the cars had stopped when the G.P.S. stopped moving so they couldn't risk passing them. They had been seen by two or three of the doormen and this could put Donny at risk.

The doormen had all left Donny's car and stood in a row with the other four taking a piss.

"High tide tonight lads!" Mick said followed by a whistle. He turned and saw Donny still sat in the car. "Too posh to piss with the rest of us Donny?" A few laughed and joined in with the 'pick on the new kid' routine.

"He's scared to get out his tiny pecker! Scared to stand next to the big boys!"

Donny felt like he was losing his appeal. Since leaving the club he'd remained pretty quiet and felt he was risking any small influence he may have. If he was going to have any swing on leading his hunting party away from Geordie, Kenny and Brit he was going to have to step up his roleplay. He stood and walked over to the row of men and jumped over the verge, now he was facing all the men. He pulled down his zip and joined the doormen's efforts.

"Just didn't want you to see your mam's name tattooed on my cock Mick. But seeing as you invited me so kindly."

The men began to laugh, and Ray nudged Mick in appreciation of taking some banter back. The doormen started to finish up as Mick piped up again.

"So why did you move to the area again Donny?"

All the men threw their eyes back at Donny as he stood with himself still exposed. He finished up and zipped up his trousers.

"Work, mate, there is nothing up north, so me and the wife thought we should take a gamble and see if I could get in at the steelworks in Scunthorpe."

Mick's eyes stayed locked on his.

"Well, have you? They have a pretty tight workforce there, many stay there till retirement. It's a big gamble." Mick was pushing and Donny felt he was still suspicious of him from the break room at the club. As comfortably as he could Donny replied,

"It's looking good, I'm just waiting for a reply from them. The wife has family here though. I think she felt safer taking a gamble if she had a bit more of a safety net in place."

Mick smiled. "Well, good luck mate, why don't you travel the rest of the way with me and Ray? I know he'll want to start talk strategy with you for the hunt."

"Sure," said Donny.

Mick motioned for one of the men in his car to jump out and get in the car behind as he approached to take his place. He looked at Donny like he was crud as he passed for the imposition. Donny gave a deep exhale before getting into the car. He knew the next hour was going to be another round of storytelling.

Ian contacted Wilson that Donny had started moving again. He asked that they stay at the end of the track until he checked the map. This was heading to the buildings that Platty had noticed on the map. The track was about 17 miles but seemed to stop well short of the buildings. Tony and Wilson took the time they had to get into their uniforms and camouflage up; this took them about ten minutes. At the same time, they grabbed a quick bite to eat. Wilson contacted the other teams and asked if they were in position and double checked everyone was happy with the situation. Everyone replied with no problems, except Glen. As expected, his reply was, "Let's get this party started!" Glen always came out with this type of saying, but he was always on the ball.

Ian got back to Tony and Wilson informing them to go to grid 2431/3511 and head west. He could remember the area quite vividly after studying the map so gave them further instructions.

"Keep on the road you are on now, take the second left on to the B216 for about two miles, this will bring you to a small farmhouse called Hill Side Cottage. There is a wood just passed it, if you can hide the car there and I will have it picked up tomorrow. From there you will be on foot, this will knock about seven miles off your journey. Don't worry lads, I will keep you right, with the tracker." His recollection of the area was invaluable, and Wilson was glad he had asked for his help.

After about 15 minutes they could see the cottage, they slowed down to see if there was any sign of life in it or around the area. There was nothing so Wilson and Tony continued to the wood. They stopped at the far end, checking as they passed to see if there was a low hanging tree to hide the car. There were none so they parked on a farm track leading to a field. They got out leaving the doors open, both stood still and quiet listening for any sound. Tony and Wilson looked at one another and then gave the thumbs up. They quietly closed the doors and headed to the back of the wood, looking all the time for a gap to hide the car. It had to be well hidden, with the farm being so close. Wilson spotted one, it was about two threads down the side of the wood and it went deep into the thicket. Tony agreed, checking back at the location of the car. They would have to come through the gate to the fields as they headed back to the car. Wilson kept checking the ground, it would be foolish to leave any tracks. As they got back to the car everything looked quite still and the track looked good. The gate was not locked so Tony got into the car, started it up and Bob opened the gate. Tony left the lights off and Wilson walked in front. The car was hardly making a sound as Tony just let it tick over and when it was needed, he gave it just enough throttle to keep it going. Tony had been on more driving courses than you could dream of. He was a top driver and there was nothing you could tell him about driving or about cars.

As soon as the car was in the wood, Wilson went back and closed the gate. He brushed over the tracks to hide any sign that a car had been there. When he got back to the vehicle Tony was taking his time with getting branches off the trees, careful not to make a noise. Although they were about a hundred metres past the farmhouse they knew, all farms have dogs and dogs can hear for miles. Wilson give a hand with the last bits when he had finished covering the tracks. They both knew to look for the freshest trees as they didn't make a lot of noise when you snap them.

The car was hidden. The equipment was checked and packed. Wilson radioed back to Ian and told him the location of the car and keys hidden on the rear tyre chassis. The radio was turned down low. Wilson and Tony began to move in.

17: Arrival

I was on the end of the mattress and kept looking at the door. It would be opened soon and I expected things to get loud and painful. I knew we would not be released without one more kicking – for old time's sake – by Prat Peter and Stevie dumb fuck. I had just started to feel like I could fight back again, however, I couldn't work out whether or not to take it if they started, or fight back.

Voices were outside of the shed, I got up and looked though the gap in the doors. There were two men, I couldn't make out who, but I could hear what was being said. They were sick of having to be the ones that have to stay at the shed and look after the cars. I went back to the mattresses and lay down looking at the roof of the hut, just thinking what had I done to end up here; Kenny and Brit lay quiet, probably thinking the same.

More cars started pulling up, we had lost count of how many men had got out of them. Sitting back down we went over the plan, again. We all agreed to try and get as much time in distance between us and them, if they are going to give us that time to run. Kenny sighed and puffed as he went along with us but I knew he still had reservations about us breaking up once we got out there.

We heard another car pull up, got up to have a look though the gap in the door. It was like we were waiting for our execution. Brit got there first and me and Kenny stood next to him. We hoped it was no more men, just supplies but no.

"It looks like four in this one lads, and there is a second car coming down the track, four in that one too," said Brit.

Everyone got out of the first car and started hugging and shaking hands, just as second car pulled up. Two of the lads out of the first car turned and opened the doors for the occupants in the second.

"NO FUCKING WAY!!" cried Brit. He didn't believe his swollen eyes, *"NO WAY!"* he said, shaking his head. "I don't believe it, fuck me!" I could see in Brit's face that he was in pure disbelief.

"What is it Brit?" I asked as I moved to the crack in the door.

"Geordie, look at them and tell me if I am right."

Something had startled Brit, I had to check it out. The light was not good but with the car headlights we could see enough.

"SHIT! What is he doing with them?" I said.

Kenny was starting to get frustrated; we hadn't said what it was we couldn't believe. I turned to Kenny. "It's Donny, he's *with* them!"

"Who the fuck is *Donny*?" Kenny asked.

"58 Donny." I saw Kenny trying to work out who we were talking about. He knew Donny by sight but hadn't much to do with him at base. I couldn't work out what was going on. Had Donny set us up at the club? Was he in with this twisted circle of men who took part in the hunt? The shock and questions spun in my mind forcing my legs to take me down closer to the floor until I had my bearings again.

"Do you think Donny is in on this Brit?" I asked.

Brit looked as if he'd put more order to what we had just seen. His face had relaxed a little and in spite of (like me and Kenny) being a subject of paranoia and perplexing ideas, our cabin fever had cast upon us, Brit had held on to reality more than I had.

"No, Donny wouldn't do that, he is one of the lads, one of *us*. He has got to be looking for us, infiltrating the doormen to find out where we are." Brit left us with the idea of hope. The silence in the shed lasted only a few moments but it powered up our drive to get through this night. We didn't know how many of our lads were with him, if any at all, but we took the small comfort that we had help.

"This changes everything! What do we do?" asked Kenny.

"We stick to the plan. None of us can let on we know Donny. If he's managed to infiltrate the bastards we have got to trust that he has a plan himself," answered Brit. I had trained with Donny, talked and drank with him. He was always a good lad and I had always respected him, but the paranoia always took my final thought.

"If we are wrong, what will we do?" I asked.

Brit looked at me like I had burst the bubble of hope he had managed to carefully nurture over the last few minutes.

"We stick to the plan Geordie. If Donny is with them I'm sure he will let us know, he will be the first to say and he will call us by name, but until that moment we make sure we say nothing. He may have used his link to us as a way of getting in or he may be playing them. We can keep a little suspicion but don't blow any chance we have in case he is on our side. Donny is good in the field, we could use that right now."

Brit was right, he knew Donny and had only been close to people he trusted, Donny had been one of them. I had to trust his feeling on this and hope more of our lads are out there looking for us.

We sat huddled by the door for a few more minutes and watched the men go into the next shed. We waited until it was clear that Donny and the doormen weren't coming out anytime soon. They were no doubt having a good chat with Big Bob and going over the schedule for the next few days. We moved back over to the slightly more comfortable mattresses.

We all sat silent playing out the scenarios the arrival of Donny had inspired. Kenny broke the noiselessness with the logic that me and Brit really needed right now.

"He wouldn't go through a war with us, train and fight with us just to betray two of his mates and join in with this hunt. Arseholes like that can't make it in the army, they don't sit silently holding this perversion while working hard and getting on with the rest of us. They go A.W.O.L. and let their issues fester by the day not stay at base with the rest of us. These bastards have none of the respect or loyalty our lads do." He looked at me and Brit straight in the eyes.

"Donny is with us."

Interlude

WILDERNESS

My father never spoke much to me. To be honest I never thought I knew or understood him. He wanted me to succeed, I never questioned that but I never thought it had anything to do with his love for me as his son. More as a proof of his character to others.

I had muddled through life. Choices, actions, thoughts and regrets never giving me any answers. If anything, only providing me with more. Clarity and wisdom came with experience but I rarely remembered it in anything following.

The truth is no one really knows what they are doing. The reason: choice. It's our biggest gift and unfortunate adversary and stops us from reaching the complete state of respect for ourselves and each other.

We do not yet have the true comprehension of respect as with it comes balance. A perfect equilibrium which governs our fate. Only the wilderness has this. Everything falls into place for a reason and will thrive or fall as natural selection takes effect. We like to think we act the same way. But like our understanding of the universe, it is small and juvenile.

The wilderness knows our strengths and our weaknesses. We either find balance with it or we don't make it out.

No measure of man comes from his choices alone but his respect of this balance, respect of our wilderness.

He never told me he loved me, nor did I say it to him. The last time I saw him alive he held my hand and looked at me with the eyes that showed his understanding. He understood everything. For those brief moments I understood to.

He was my wilderness and I was his.

18: Positions

Dunc and his team had set off and headed in the direction of the buildings that were on the map in the centre of the swamp. The land was rough and unforgiving. It was taking more time than he wished to spend to cover. They had been on foot for about three hours and felt it was time to stop and have a quick rest and to check the map.

Dunc, Glen, Platty and Jock were covering the north side of the swamp, they were around two hours away from position, the hopeful direction that me, Kenny and Brit would be heading to. Tony and Bob Wilson would be holding the south close to the buildings me and the lads were being held. They had made good timing and got to about 400 metres off the shed, they took cover behind a small mound. Ian's men were holding east and west while Ian coordinated at OPS 1 at base.

The early morning light would be up soon and the teams were keen for the assistance in the swamp's terrain but light brought apprehension, it was the time the hunt would begin and the eyelines of the enemy would also become clearer. I could hear the doormen having a good laugh at the expense of me and my two good mates. I would say Steve seemed to be the one with the big mouth, it seemed he was trying to impress the doormen from down south; this got to Kenny.

"I am going to kill the fucking cunt as soon as I see him!"

Me and Brit laughed.

"You are in no shape, Rocket, you couldn't fuck shit!" Brit said, but to be fair, Kenny was looking a lot better than he had been. His eye was open and the swelling had gone down a lot. The cut Brit had made still looked raw and painful, the blood had scabbed around it and mixed with the sweat and muck. I thought it did looked infected, but with his spirits high, he could fight through the pain and we would worry about that later.

The time was getting on, it had to be about 05:00 hours, the sun was coming up, and it had all gone a bit quiet in the shed next door.

Donny hadn't said a lot when he was sitting in the shed, he was listening to the doormen, sussing out if any of them had plans on how to track us. He thought that two of them seemed to be well up on tactics, it seemed that they had done this before. He continued listening and asking the odd question, and so it came out that one of the doormen, Dave, had been in the Paras.

He had started to tell a story, about when he was in the army. Just as he did Donny stood up and shouted,

"YOU'RE A FUCKING KNOB, I am here to get them twats next door and you are no better than them!"

Big Bob stood up and grabbed Donny, Dave got up ready to take him on, then it all seemed to kick off, everyone seemed to be up trying to stop one another from getting to each other. When Donny put up his hands in submission. Dave seemed to do the same and the room calmed down. Dave looked at Donny.

"That is why I am no longer a Para," he said, "I can't stand the dicks."

Big Bob was still standing, and informed them all about

Donny's mate. Dave stood back up and put his hand out to Donny, Donny shook his hand and apologised.

"No problem mate," he said. "If you would like to come with me on the hunt you can, I have a better chance of catching them than this lot." As he looked around the room he laughed and they all started to boo him. Donny looked at Big Bob, "No disrespect to you mate, but I will go with Dave if that's ok. I think as he has been one of them, he should think like them and get to the three lads quicker than the rest of you." Donny said this with a wink.

Bob laughed. "Not a problem mate, but you will not get there before my team, we are the best."

Everyone started to brag on how good each other was and the taunts and sneers were met with laughter and bigger sneers as the packs finished up with their food. Donny hoped his last outburst had gained him a little more ball cred, but at the same time he knew Dave was a threat to his mission. He knew he'd have to stick close to him and put Dave down at the earliest opportunity he could. Hopefully the charade would have also convinced Mick. Donny knew once the hunt began he'd have to keep a close eye on him. He felt his doubt over his loyalty since the club; he wasn't sure if Mick had finally clicked to where he'd seen Donny before and was keeping him going long enough till the hunt started to throw him to the wolves as well.

I thought we would be kept in the shed for another day as the daylight crept through the gaps of the building. The days were becoming more and more agonising. As our bodies were mending our minds were beginning to cripple.

I assumed they would not be letting us out until dark, but then we heard the lock being tampered with. Billy entered sheepishly with two of the lads that had come through the night. They had another tray of food.

"Morning lads," Billy said to his chest.

We all just sat on the mattresses and didn't say a word, just put our hands up to shield our eyes from the morning sun. They put the trays down on the floor, it looked as if it was cornflakes and a cup of tea.

Brit piped up. "Thank you, waiter," he said. "You can all go now, so we can have a shower…oh, and Billy, can you bring me some shampoo please."

Me and Kenny couldn't help but laugh. You could see Billy getting upset, he was red in the face and must have been instructed not to touch us. Not that I felt he ever would. Out of all the men we had seen Billy was their weakest link. He had told us that he didn't normally do this kind of thing. We hadn't seen him alone, if we had I know I would have tried to work him on freeing us. Maybe Big Bob knew his commitment to the hunt and that's why he was never allowed to see us solo. But I had always suspected it was Billy who had left the bag of gear in the rafters of the shed for us to find.

Billy seemed to cover his embarrassment by ignoring what Brit had said. "You haven't met my two mates have you?" he said. "This is Rob," pointing to the one on his left, "and this is Dave" pointing to the one on his right.

Dave walked towards us, bent down and had a good look at Kenny's eye. "That looks bad, does it hurt mate?" as he pressed his thumb into the cut.

Kenny knocked his hand away, and looked right into his eyes. "Not as much as yours will when I get the chance to get you all back for this," he whispered.

Dave stood up and laughed.

"What makes you think you will get the chance?" he said.

Kenny looked at me. I give him the look, to hold back and not give them a reason to knock us about. He turned his head and looked back at Dave then lowered it in submission. Dave walked away.

"That one is mine at the start line," Dave said to Billy as he passed.

Kenny's eye had opened up again. Blood trickled down his cheek but he never blinked nor wiped away the stream. He kept his eyes locked on Dave's back. As they left, Kenny put his hands over it, he never said a word but me and Brit could tell he was in a lot of pain. Brit had a good look at it.

"Not too bad mate it will stop soon." He could see as well as me, that the blood was mixed with puss, it was infected.

Tony had been looking out though the mound he and Wilson waited at, they were about 300 metres from the buildings he thought his lads were in. They were up a slight verge, concealed by some thick blackberry bushes and high conifers. His binoculars fixed steady at the entry points of the two buildings. He had seen men come out of one hut and go into the other. He gave Wilson a nudge. "Three have gone from the hut on the left into the one on the right and one of them was carrying a tray of food in looked like."

Wilson looked through his binoculars. "I'll get onto the lads with the grid reference of the hut our lads are in."

Tony started to check out the lay of the land that was to the front of the huts, specifically in the direction of the swamp. After a few minutes Wilson made his way back to where Tony crouched.

"It's like the Falklands terrain," said Tony.

Wilson looked again at the panorama around the huts. "All tufts and lumps of grass, hard to run in, we'll have to watch where we put our feet."

All of the lads had checked in with Ian and everyone was ready to go. Glen got on the radio to Tony and asked if he could see anything.

"Not at the moment mate, but we have seen three of them and it looks like they are giving the lads food," said Tony.

"If it is Geordie and the lads," Glen replied, "you make sure you keep me informed, mate."

Tony knew Glen was concerned for Kenny more than Geordie and Brit. When Kenny joined the regiment, Glen had taken him under his wing and looked after him. Glen was not going to let any of them get away if they hurt them, especially Kenny. Brit and Dunc were the same as Kenny and Glen. From day one when Brit joined the regiment if you took on him, you took on Dunc as well, no matter where or when, Dunc and Brit would be together.

Back at Glen's location, Jock had started to dig a shell scrape with Platty, checking the location of where they were on the map to the location of the huts. Dunc and Glen, had decided to do a second shell scrape about 50 metres away from the first and back away about 50 metres of line so if they had to stay at that location, should any of the packs come in their direction, they would have a chance of ambushing them.

After they had completed the two shell scrapes, Glen took Platty and headed in the direction of the huts. They set up three trip flares, about 150 metres apart.

Platty couldn't understand why Glen had put them in the location he had. "Why have you done this mate?"

Glen looked at him. "Look at the location they will be coming from. Look at the location we will be at. Now look at the location of the three trip flares."

Platty understood the locations but shook his head still looking puzzled, unable to see the logic.

"Well, if the lads come in this direction, from the hut, they will hit this one." Glen pointed to the one in front, "and they will change direction, head to this one" pointing to the second one, "and that will send them off to the third one which will send them in the direction of us. If this all goes to plan. Then they should head for your shell scrape. That is when me and Dunc can come up from behind them, and you and Jock come from in front."

Platty put the strategy together and felt a little foolish. Glen hadn't showed any judgement in his tone. He was extraordinarily good at tactics, and his brain could work out pattern and movements. For sure he was trained by some native American Indian chief thought Platty. The imaginary feathered headdress brought a split-second grin to Platty's face.

"I have one or two things in my backpack for you and Jock. I think you will like them," said Glen.

They headed back to Dunc and Jock, who had put a cuppa on. Glen crouched down next to Dunc and started to talk out a plan. In situations like this you always have a plan, you may not get to use it but it is always safe to have one. Glen started to inform them of the layout of the trip flares, and why it would hopefully cause a bit of panic and collapse their defence.

"Hopefully these arseholes won't have come up with anything like this; *this* will put the shits up them and put them on the back foot." Glen then went into his backpack and pulled out a length of chain. At one end, it had a wooden handle, at the other there was about eight metal spikes. Glen handed it to Jock. "Do you know how to use it mate?"

Jock's eyes lit up like he had been given an early Christmas gift.

"Yes! I will bray the fuck out of them with it!" he laughed.

Glen frowned and started to get annoyed.

"Don't fuck about mate, shit is starting to get real. I don't know for sure but I would say the lads on the hunt are going to be big and most of them will be up for a fight, so don't fuck on. From now on we have to be ready and in the right frame of mind."

They all looked at Glen and knew he was right. If they didn't switch on to this they will not come out on top. Glen took back the chain.

"Always try to hit them with the end of it, mate. If you try to hit them with the middle of it, you will only give them a chance of grabbing it. The end of it will rip their faces off. We can assume not all of them will have firing weapons. Hand to hand will be useful if we need to be discreet with our sounds so not to alert the other packs."

Jock stood up and started to give it a go. His swings were not elegant, but he had force which would make the difference.

"You have it Jock," Glen said. "Now sit down, see what I have for Platty." In his backpack he pulled out an old police truncheon. "This is what I took off a copper in Scunny. You should be ok with that, mate." He handed it to Platty.

"Heavier than I thought," said Platty as he hit it into his hands.

Dunc looked at Glen, "Well? What's in your Mary Poppin's bag for me mate?"

"Just a Machete mate, can you handle it?" said Glen handing the wide 15-inch blade to Dunc.

"That will do just fine," said Dunc.

"Right lads, let's start to get in position and sort out a rota for the watch. Two hours at a time. I'll take first watch while yous gets some rest." With Glen's word, the others settled down in the scrape. Each studying their new weapons. Glen watches for a few minutes into the early morning light. With no signs of life, he reaches into his backpack and pulls out a ball of string which was tied at one end to a stick. He looks over to the lads seeing Jock at the furthest end of the dug-out scrape. He carefully rolls out the ball of string to him, which gently comes to a stop as it hits Jock's hip.

"Roll it out mate and take the other end to the next shell scrape. When we start to get our heads down, one from each scrape needs to have it tied to a finger, so we can communicate without sound, two pulls at a time to wake up, two pulls as a reply you are awake, then one for people in sight." They all nodded. *The Message* we called it. It was what we did in the Falklands, simple but an effective silent alarm.

Bob Wilson was on look out. He checked his watch. 05:37, the early morning sun was still dull, as if the swamp's abundance of moisture in the air had diluted its strength. Tony only a few moments ago had put his head down. Wilson knew he would not be sleeping but 30 minutes of silence could perform wonders when out in the field. Wilson knew his men were ready for what was to come. He knew them well and respected each of them. As the highest rank on this mission, he had absolute commitment to its success. He had tried to analyse every possibility and eventuality of the mission, as he had done for days now. He was exhausted. Sleep had eluded him since Tony first came to him with the news of the disappearance of Geordie, Kenny and Brit. The only things that had kept him going was his 30 a day habit, cold strong tea, as well as the thought of justice. Justice, being a pacifist's term for revenge. Truth was, Wilson loved a fight. A few drinks with a few new recruits always lead to his authority being slightly abused when he'd draft an overly keen-to-impress freshman into a brawl on a night out. Never for any serious harm, only the thrill. This fight was different, he knew some of his men would get hurt, some may never make it back to base … and that scared the shit out of him.

He paced the rugged ground occasionally grabbing one of the thorny blackberry stems to get a jolt of adrenalin pumping. When something caught his eye. A quick flash of light. He raised his binoculars and saw a strong beam of light from the inside of the doormen's hut reflect off one of the car's windscreens. He nudged Tony with his foot and signalled him to take a look.

Tony got straight up and looked over the mound. He could not see a lot as he was disorientated from a brief limbo into sleep. His eyes rolled back and forth registering all he saw.

There were 22 men. They all stood around six foot four. Built like brick shithouses. They positioned themselves into a large circle while three headed to the other hut.

This was it. The hunt was on.

19: The Silent Alarm

Jonny Morgan was an excellent fighter. He had been Kenny's role model through his time with Hartlepool's under 21's boxing tournaments. He was fast and powerful, always managing to knock Kenny on his arse and plenty others too. The day before the 1972 U.K championship Jonny had got himself into a fight with his brother and got a black eye. It had swollen pretty bad and he made Kenny slice his eyelid with his dad's Swiss army knife to reduce the swelling so he could compete. He did it and Jonny won the competition. After two days on his celebratory bender Jonny collapsed in Tammy's Chippy. His eye had become infected and given him blood poisoning. He died of sepsis two weeks later.

Kenny's face was burning. The pain in his eye had travelled across his whole face. His teeth ached and he felt like all the exterior swelling to his face had inverted within putting heavy pressure inside his head. He wouldn't tell Geordie or Brit. He had to stay strong for them. But he knew their plan was no longer an option. He was beginning to lose sight in his left eye, this had come on too fast and he knew that by the end of the day his vision would be gone. He would not be able to capture any of the vehicles and take out anyone who was left. He'd be killed and they'd be killed following through with the plan having nobody waiting for them.

He didn't remember Donny, but he had lied to the others when he told them he would be on their side. He knew they couldn't take another setback and thought hope would be better for them than reality. Kenny knew the only thing he could do to keep the lads alive, would be to provoke the doormen enough to get himself killed. Make them lose their shit on him so much that they would end his life, but in turn to leave the others alone to run in the hunt. He needed to give them their best shot in staying alive. This was the new plan; he'd have to make sure he did a good enough job to not be a liability, no life left to drag around the moors. He had to do this for them. He had to do this for his brothers.

"On your feet lads, let's get limbered up."

Kenny had got me and Brit up to move about and loosen our joints up once again. We were stiff and still in a bit pain but we knew we had to do it to have a chance of getting away and to take another kicking, if it was to come again.

I was getting warmed up and feeling a little more like myself again. I needed things to start. I needed out of this shed. The smell from our primitive lavatory system had become nearly unbearable and the local fly population were too comfortable with our company. My skin needed fresh air and to be revived with a splash of cold water. But most importantly, I needed to take a swing at these bastards. I had kept my anger in check for too long. They needed to pay for this and even if I died trying, I'd be happy taking a few of them to hell with me.

Just then the door on the shed opened. This time it was different, no one came in and the door was opened to its widest capacity. Steve and 'the prat' had wedged it open and now looked in.

"Time for some fun lads. Are you coming out to play?"

'The prat' walked away from the door as he said this, and was laughing as he went.

I looked at Kenny and Brit. I could see the fear in their faces, my face was probably the same. I swallowed hard.

"This is it lads," I said. "Remember, we are all in it together, if one of us is getting a kicking do not try to help, it will only make it worse."

We all stood up and stepped out into the sun. I could not see anything. The world outside was bright. Too bright to make anything out. My hand reached up to shelter my eyes and after a few moments I could see all the doormen. I felt Kenny brush past my arm to step in front of me.

"Wait," I said as I clutched his arm. he was hot, and his shirt felt damp. The natural light gave me full resolution to Kenny's face. He looked ill, his skin grey and clammy. I knew he'd been beaten hard but he looked really bad. My eyes left his face when I noticed Donny standing about three metres behind Kenny's right shoulder. He was looking directly at me but I scanned around so I didn't give him my sole focus. On second pass, he gave me a split second wink. Checking he hadn't been seen, he gave a second one. That confirmed it for me, he was with us. That meant the lads had to be out there somewhere to help us. I turned to Kenny and Brit and grabbed them as if to hug them and quietly whispered,

"Donny is with us."

All the doormen started to laugh.

"That's right! You big puffs, say goodbye to your boyfriends!" Big Bob said. "You won't see them again after today."

At that, two of the unknown doormen came and grabbed

me; I was dragged into the middle of the circle they stood in. They threw me to the floor. I got straight back to my feet and the two stepped forward again and looked at one another, inviting the other to strike first. I knew what was going to happen, in came a right hand from the one on the left. I just seen it coming and I managed to ride it to soften the blow. I stumbled back one or two paces, tripped and hit the floor. I heard Kenny's voice start to belt out all the curses he had held in the last few days and then he was silent as one of the men held a six-inch dagger at Brit's throat.

"MOUTH OFF AGAIN YOU LITTLE FAGGOT AND I'LL SLIT YOUR BOYFRIEND'S PRETTY THROAT!"

I got back to my feet, stood tall, and stared at them knowing I was going to get another kicking but I was not going to let them think I was scared, but I was. Kenny and Brit looked on, held by the threat of a very sharp blade. The second punch came from the right straight to the side of my head, I was quick enough to ride that one too but I staggered back. I turned and looked straight back at him, as if to say, *enjoy it mate, because when I get the chance I am going to kill you.* I could see in his eyes, he was shocked that I took the punch, and I had the nerve to look back at him. That was my mistake, I should have gone down and played on it.

I had to take it for Brit and Kenny. Three of them kicked me from my back, belly and crotch. They did not stop and the pain lasted until Big Bob took his size 12 Dr Martens to my face.

I heard voices, loud and all at once. Ribbons of light flew past my eyes. They went round and round, faster and faster.

"I'm gonna be sick, I'm gonna be sick" I called but I

couldn't hear the sound of my own voice. Suddenly my chest was warm and wet, my throat burned. I wasn't me. I wasn't here. I wasn't anyone.

20: Thirty Minutes

They kicked Geordie non-stop for seventeen seconds. Donny watched, biting his lip harder and harder. Ray looked at him. "Told you that you'd enjoy it!" He stepped forward in the circle. *"Woah, woah, woah* boys! Leave some life in him for the rest of us." Ray reached down and Donny saw Geordie's new mangled face as he lifted it. Blood and flesh hung from a wide opening just under his nose. Ray looked up at Big Bob. Bob nodded.

"Thirty minutes," he said as he turned and walked back to the hut.

"You heard the man, arseholes; you've got a thirty-minute headstart to get outta' here." Ray looked back down to Geordie. "Take him or leave him boys but if he's still there in half an hour his will be the first throat I slit."

Brit was thrown to the floor and Kenny ran over to Geordie. Donny stood wanting to blow everything to help his friend. But the price was too high. He'd have to suck this up. The time would come but not yet. He just hoped Geordie would be there to see it end with him.

The circle of men started to stamp, some clapped their hands slowly while others banged the weapons they had in their hands. They started to chant.

"RUN!" "RUN!" "RUN!"

The rumble of sound grew louder and louder. Kenny pulled up my left arm and pulled it over his right shoulder.

A moment later Brit was at the other arm pulling it onto his left one. With all their strength they got me to my feet and started to move towards the gap Big Bob had left in the circle of men. They pushed forward. Not looking at anyone but their target. They could not stop until they reached somewhere to hide, somewhere to lay me down safely.

Kenny's head was spinning, he thought he could have walked out there and take the beating for us, but he was not the strong one, everyone could see that. It was never going to be him they picked. The knife at Brit's throat he had not thought of, how could he have been so stupid? It was too late now. He could not waste any time with stupid invasive self-pity.

Donny watched and chanted with the packs, he watched as Kenny and Brit struggled to drag Geordie off. But he felt relief as he saw them get out of sight. Swallowed by the moors. '*Run lads,*' he thought. '*Don't stop.*'

Wilson and Tony stood powerless. They watched as one of their men took the beating of his life. They had to fight their urges to intervene. The Regiment Sergeant Major had granted them men and use of the base's facilities if they brought this hunt down and the organisers to justice. It was hard to see the big picture and keep cool when there was men you knew taking a beating for 'the greater good'. Wilson had the duty of feeding a running commentary of the incident over the radio. All teams listened in rage and disbelief.

Tony kept quiet, but was seething. Wilson made him keep eyes on Geordie, Kenny and Brit and relay their heading to the other teams, while he kept lookout at the hut.

Dunc knew it would be some time before they got anywhere near his location, but it didn't stop him getting the lads together and letting them know what had just happened. It hit Jock hard. Just before the Falklands, we had been on a course together and had got to know each other well. He had got himself in a fight one night down town and I had helped him out. From then he always said, "I won't forget this Geordie, you saved me, and I will one day pay you back." Jock never thought it would be in a situation like this. Glen calmed him down as they all sat waiting for Dunc to give them more information.

Tony observed as the men watched me, Kenny and Brit go out of sight. They went back into the hut and reappeared moments later carrying their apparent weapons of choice. Tony had to move further down a small gully to see his three men head into the direction of the swamp. He noticed I was dropping in and out of consciousness as he saw my head rise and fall. Kenny and Brit struggled to help and navigate the terrain, but they wouldn't leave me.

It had been about twenty minutes since we had been given the head start. I didn't have the ability to perceive time just yet, but I began to come around and heard the heavy breaths and conversation of Kenny and Brit, and felt my arse and thighs drench from being set down on the damp moorland. My body felt tight and my face hurt beyond my limited comprehension. I had thought I'd be used to feeling like this, but the new reminder showed me how much a good kicking can break even the strongest of men. I could only hope the same level of pain wasn't with Kenny and Brit as well.

"Are you two ok?" I said with a hoarse voice.

"We're just fine, you big soft shite," said Kenny as he crouched down next to me. He checked me over, while Brit kept lookout. "You'll not win any beauty pageants, Geordie, but you never would have anyway." Kenny smiled. "Can you move Geordie? We're not safe yet."

My limbs felt like they didn't belong to my body but I managed to stand upright, though I felt as weak as a kitten. Brit looked over. "We need to keep moving, Geordie I know you feel like shit but if we can make it over to the thicket further down you'll be able to have a few minutes to pull yourself together."

I nodded as the lads took to each side of me. We started slow, but as adrenalin began to fuel my body again we picked up the pace. The thicket of bushes passed us as momentum kept us going. We all knew nowhere was safe, we had to move out as far as we could.

Tony and Wilson kept a check on the hut and called all stations to inform them of the direction we had started to head. Two of the back-up teams had moved closer into the swamp. They had gone to the high areas. From there they could look down and see any movement. They would report back to camp as it had been agreed they would only get involved if things got out of hand and the two teams couldn't handle it. Ian would then be able to work out what team was in the area and who would be in the best location to lay cover.

Tony tapped Wilson on the shoulder and pointed to the huts, there was movement. It had only been 25 minutes since the start but all of the doormen had come out and stood in one big group. Tony worked out who was in charge as the largest of the men stood at the front. His coat was opened and looked like it was padded out, most likely with his personal arsenal of weapons. He seemed to be sorting them into groups. As the men started to divide, it seemed there would be five teams of four men. The two men remaining headed back into the hut; they must be staying behind to look after things and possibly to take the cars to a pickup point at the end of the hunt.

32 minutes had passed, the groups had been arranged. The weapons had been chosen. Donny looked out into the hazy moorland. He stood with Ray, Mick and the ex Para Dave. They had decided to bear left from where the lads had headed, Donny's idea. He'd noticed Kenny had struggled more with the weight of my body which had affected their drag to bear left slightly.

It had begun. Two teams had set off, Big Bob had staggered each team.

This was it.

21: Broken Forge

Ian felt like a spare part. He knew the equipment better than most men at the base, but as zero hour for the hunt began he had wanted nothing more than to be out at the moors. They had kept him informed and knowing the area he felt as though he could step into the map and visualise all around him. He had always been a 'doer' and being so he always felt it easier to get the job done himself. He knew and trusted all the men out there on the mission, but if anything went wrong he knew he'd have to live with the 'what ifs?' and he'd deal with them hard.

The tracker on Donny's location had remained still. It was now 40 minutes since Wilson had called in, telling them Geordie, Brit and Kenny had set off. He paced the ground in front of the display. The cheap carpet floor tiles were worn through. He started to think of how many Majors had done the same. How many hours spent and miles covered on the same six tiles. The pressure cooker kept its name up. The room was humid and the stench of stale sweat added to its displeasure. But its hell was still better than what his men were facing.

Wilson's voice echoed the still room.

"*IAN*, Donny is on the move. Come back."

Ian watched the monitor as his signal began to coordinate with his movements.

"I am tracking Donny, standby."

Ian focused on the screen, willing its servers to keep up. "He should be about 600 metres to the east of you and Tony, is that right?"

A moment passed and Wilson confirmed it.

Ian sat back at the desk and pulled his map closer. He began to mark the coordinates of Donny's movement.

"Here we go."

Tony asked if they should hit the hut first, or go after Donny's group. Wilson thought it best to leave the huts as there could be more than two men inside.

"We should go after Donny's group, that way we have an even chance. He may run into Geordie soon and that needs to be our priority, while those men are at bay."

Tony checked the map and noticed the gully he had been up earlier, ran for about three miles in the direction they headed. If they could get in front of Donny's group they could ambush them. If they could take them out it would give them a hell of a lot more freer movement. If they got in the sightlines of any of the other doormen groups, they would hopefully not be recognised from a distance.

The gully wasn't as deep as they thought, but it did give a bit of cover. After about 25 minutes Tony popped up and had a look. He quickly got back down as the group was a lot closer than he had expected. They had to be about 50 metres away. Tony signalled Wilson to take a look. Wilson lay behind a small mound, and had a good look all around. There was only the one group, Donny's. He got back in the gully and looked to Tony.

"We'll head up another ten minutes to get in front of them."

Tony nodded.

Wilson was thinking how to approach this while they travelled silently ten minutes through the gully.

Tony had a second look. This time Donny's group had to be about a 1\4 mile behind them. Wilson took a second look, he always liked to doublecheck things to be on the safe side. He took off his backpack and radio and told Tony to do the same.

"This is it mate, we have to go for them."

Tony nodded and stared with determination at Wilson. He followed Wilson's lead and opened his combat jacket and rolled up the sleeves.

"We are going to walk out towards them. Hopefully, they will think we are poaching for rabbits."

Tony had a fold-up shovel; he got it out and clicked it together. He took off his pack and got out a flannel from his wash bag, and wiped the camouflage cream off his face. He handed it to Wilson and he did the same. They both tried to look casual as they set off. Tony had the shovel over his shoulder while Wilson had a machete strapped to his waist.

"Who the fuck are these dicks?" said Mick.

Donny had already spotted the familiar forms of Wilson and Tony rise up from his left but remained silent, for one of the others to spot. In the meanwhile, he moved slightly behind Mick, who walked at the rear of the group. It wouldn't take long for Ray and Mick to recognise the new visitors to the swamp. They had visited the club twice looking for the hunters' playthings and now were on the moors by coincidence. Donny knew his roleplay was soon to be at an end and things were soon going to get messy.

Ray signalled his team to stop. "Me and Dave will go check these fuckers out. Mick, you and Donny stay here and keep lookout." Ray hung a longer look at Mick, "You alright with that mate?"

"Sure thing big lad," said Mick.

Ray and Dave headed forward to Wilson and Tony. Time slowed as Donny thought how to play this.

As the distance closed it revealed Donny's teammates. The woolly hat had disguised the identity of Ray, the head doorman at the club. Wilson bit his lip, questioning his stupidity at not realising who had been travelling with Donny. Five metres stood between the parties.

"Fancy seeing you all the way out here, Major Watson was it?" Ray said, with a smug look on his face. He turned back to Mick, "Oi, oi, Mick," he shouted. "Looks like you were right!"

Donny felt a tight grip around his neck, tighter than he expected from the man standing next to him.

"I knew I recognised you, squaddie prick."

The knife fell into Donny's body hard. The cold blade was the biggest shock but soon felt hot as the blood seeped out. When the second hand joined the first at Donny's neck he stumbled forward and the moors started to fall away.

Ray stole the attention from what was going on behind him. He and Dave stood taller than Wilson and Tony and nearly double their width.

"It's Wilson actually. We are on an exercise out here. Survival training."

Ray laughed. "Doing a bit of that ourselves."

The two stood waiting for the other to reveal their hand. Ray didn't let anything go. Wilson took a step forward while Tony took two.

"Well then, Roy was it? We'll let you get on your way,"

said Wilson as he turned slipping Tony a wink. Tony turned as if to walk away, however quickly spun 360 degrees with his shovel extended smacking Dave square in the side of his head. He collapsed to the floor. Wilson stood ready with his machete in his right hand. As Ray turned to see Dave hit the floor Wilson moved in booting the back of his calves sending him down to his knees, then a foot to his face sending Ray to meet Dave down in the ground.

Dave was down but not out, as he started to get back up Tony sent the shovel to meet the other side of his face. His head rocked back and his nose burst open as it hit a rock embedded in the soil. Tony grabbed him by the hair, and started to lay into him. Wilson checked on Ray who was out. He looked back to Tony who was making a mess of the Para. Tony had lost it and was belting him in the face releasing everything he had held in for the last few days. Wilson had known Tony for a long time and had never seen him like this. He was out of control. Wilson eased down in front of him.

"He's out cold Tony! Leave him!"

Tony stopped, reaching from breath. His fists were bright red and starting to fray at the knuckles. He took a long blink and looked up. His eyes were drawn over to a dark lump in the ground, about 30 metres ahead. It was still and alone.

"*Fuck Bob!* I think that's Donny!"

22: Refuge

Kenny Brit and me had got our heads sorted. We kept going and would stop about every two miles to check if anyone was following. Our original plan had fallen, now all we could do to stay alive was to keep going. Donny was here and we hoped he had brought some of the other lads along as well. For now, we took slight comfort in the thought of backup and focused on what we thought was the best way to continue.

Just as we had stopped for the second time we could see a group in the distance. They had to be about a good 1 1/2 miles behind us. We sat down for five minutes to get our breath back and set off again. The pain we had been in had escaped from our minds; we had to think about getting away. We knew if we got caught that would be it. We were too damaged. Kenny still looked like hell, fighting the pain of his body and what we could only imagine from the infection. This had been the first time we had been in a situation like this, even when we were down the Falklands we didn't think it was as life threatening as this. It was probably worse but when you are with all of your regiment, sergeant majors and unlimited firearms you think you can take on the whole world.

We kept going and had to help one another from time to time, but didn't stop until we all thought we had covered the two miles we agreed.

Glen and Jock had got to the top of the lookout point. They dug a shallow trench and got themselves into position. Glen took first lookout while Jock lay back in the grass just to rest his head until it was his turn to lookout. The sun had come up and its rays fell on his face. It was the closest he had felt to calm in days. But it didn't last long as Wilson's voice came over the radio. It was Donny, he was down.

Ian had to make the call. Donny was down and one of the hunters had got away with the news that the army had infiltrated the hunt. This changed everything. For now, Wilson and Tony were tending to Donny. He had lost blood and was unconscious. He needed to move two teams. One needed to pick up the two men Wilson had taken down and head back to the road with Donny, he would contact his brother to pick them up. The second had to find the rogue hunter, and raid the huts in case they put word out of our involvement. For the moment Wilson and Tony were out so for now he only had two teams on the lookout for Geordie and the lads. Ian sunk in his chair feeling more helpless than ever.

We had to stop again to get our breath back. I could feel my face starting to swell. Brit looked at me. He could tell I was struggling. My whole face had swollen; my lip had burst open, again, from my stumbles and countless lashes from passing branches and started to bleed. Kenny had a look at me. He was not as diplomatic as Brit.

"Geordie, you look shit mate, you can't continue like this."

"I don't have a choice mate, what do you want me to do? Stay here and let them catch me?" I said it but knew it was not an option.

Kenny took off his coat and ripped the lining out. He

got a handful of grass and soil then wrapped it in the lining. He got Brit to grab one end and they twisted it until water started to squeeze out of the lining. He took the cloth and wiped my face with it to try and cool me down. The soft, moist cloth felt good against my skin and perked me up for a moment. I knew I was still not right, but I took the cloth and wiped my eyes and tried to look as if I was miraculously cured. It did clear the dry blood and dirt away but my face still hurt like hell. Kenny took the cloth back, wiping my face again. His eyes squinted, creasing his forehead. Dirt mixed with sweat and collected in the creases giving the impression of deep wrinkles. His skin was pale and the natural light showed him looking gaunt. He looked about 100 years old. I'd never seen Kenny weak in all the time I knew him. And here he was again, not giving anything away of his own pain tending to mine. I'd never forget this about him.

Brit went for a look around. The land ahead of us dropped down about ten feet. This would put us out of sight for a while. Brit came back and thought we should have a decoy to put some extra distance between us and them. He put it to Kenny, "If you head off to the right and get yourself seen, you can head down that side of the hill." He pointed to the northeast. "I can get Geordie off to the left and head off around the bottom, northwest. They will hopefully head for you, then you can double back to us and we will get a bit more time away from them."

It was ridiculous. I piped up,

"NO FUCKING WAY! He isn't putting himself at risk for me! We will stick together or you leave me and get yourself away."

Kenny nodded at Brit. "Fuck it Geordie. We will make our own decisions. You'd do it for us."

At that Kenny jumped up and set off. I had no choice in the matter now. I knew it was a good idea but I hated them having to look after me. I knew they both felt like crap, Kenny more so, and would never be happy with their decision. Brit helped me to my feet and we set off in the opposite direction. As we went I could feel my bones starting to ache once more, but this time I felt as if I could handle it. Brit let go and we set off in a slow jog.

Wilson rolled Ray down into the gully meeting Dave at the bottom. He had gagged their mouths and cable tied their hands and feet. He had contacted Ian with the news and he had relayed his plan with the next step. Donny had a slow but steady pulse at the minute and Tony had stopped the bleeding. His stab wound looked like it had just hit his muscle and not snagged any of his organs. The bruises to his neck suggested he had been strangled, maybe the sight of Ray and Dave being took down had made his attacker retreat. Donny was ok for now, but they would have to move him soon. They were too exposed and waiting for assistance for an uncertain amount of time left imminent threat hanging in the air.

Dunc's group hadn't made any contact yet with any of the doormen. They were at a high point about 1/2 mile ahead keeping lookout. Glen said he would head out with Jock; if they saw anything, Jock could come and assist.

As we got down behind the rise the land seemed to be a lot flatter and easier to move over; we had started to make good time and I was thinking about Kenny. Would he catch up with us? or would he continue to head in the opposite direction? I hoped not, but I never knew for certain what Kenny would do. He was so unpredictable and took risks.

Kenny was brave but sometimes fortune does not favour this alone.

Kenny had got into the open area and could see the first group of doormen, they had to be about 1 1/2 miles away from him. He sat down and waited for them to get closer. At 3/4 of a mile away he got up, looked down at them and was waiting and hoping they would look up. He thought whether he should shout out or throw a stone at them but he thought it would be a giveaway to something not right. He was focused on his footing while moving a little further down the bank when they got their eye on him and they started shouting up at him. He made it look as if he was surprised to have been spotted as he set off to the right and back over the mound. As he got out of sight he doubled back off to the left to catch up with me and Brit. We hoped it had sent them in the wrong direction.

Tony and Wilson had set off with Donny. Tony supporting his head and shoulders while Wilson carried his feet. They headed towards Dunc's group but as yet didn't know if any of the packs lay between them. They were moving as quickly as they could across open land. In the current situation it was the best course to get to a dense line of trees which could offer a short-term refuge. They heard movement as they approached the tree line. Snapping twigs echoed within the tallness of the trees. Someone was close. They set Donny down quietly, and silently took point at either end of him. They waited.

Kenny could see us in the distance and started to pick up speed. He hadn't heard any signs of being followed. But he still kept his senses on full alert. When he caught up with us he grabbed my arm.

"You need help old man?"

I smiled back at him, sheer relief that he was still in one piece. "Fuck you, you little shit."

Kenny thought they had fallen for the bait and headed in the wrong direction. With any luck, we would not see that group again. We would be out of the moors before they even realized they were headed in the wrong direction.

Brit stopped suddenly.

"What the fuck's wrong mate?" Kenny asked.

"Look over there!" Brit pointed ahead of us.

In the distance about three or four miles ahead was woodland. We looked at each other in disbelief. Woodland isn't common in moorland. Maybe it was small but it was worth a look. It had to be about 18:00 hours as the sun had started to go down; we needed cover. With any hope the packs would start to rest soon too and we could make the most of a little down time.

23: The Woods

Dunc had started to get concerned. He had not heard any comms for hours. Platty made his way up to Glen to see if he had seen anything. But like him, nothing. He decided to radio Ian to see what, if anything, was happening. Ian had reported that no one had checked in for a while. His backup teams were out looking for Mick and the second were an hour away from raiding the huts. Donny was stable, so they were leaving him in the care of Wilson and Tony till they took care of business. They were losing light and Dunc felt they were waiting for nothing. Things were happening far away for them and at the moment the only impressions his strong team were making were with their asses on the ground. They needed to move out.

We had reached the wood. it was quite dense with small heather type bushes growing between the trees. We got there as the sun had gone down. We sat just inside of the first couple of trees. We all seemed to be down with the pain running through our bodies. The pain in my eyes had eased but I still felt like shit. We looked out over the way we had come. No one in sight but we couldn't relax, we had to be ready in case anyone headed this way. We thought it best if we sat it out overnight, taking turns to keep watch as we could be going in circles with the veil of darkness.

Denis Welsh headed the team to raid the huts. He was a B.S.M. from 9 battery. He was a hard lad from a fishing village in the Northumberland town of Amble, and had been the regiment's rugby trainer. His team had reached the huts. There were no sounds. Two of the lads crept closer to see if there were any signs of life in the area. Taff and Evo clung around the walls of the huts as if they were magnetized. The first hut was unmanned. The door was open, Evo looked in and could see a number of cars and a van. As they headed to the next hut they spotted a light shining though the gap of the double doors. They moved around the rear to listen, they could hear a conversation between what seemed to be three men. One of them had to have dropped out of the hunt as there was only two that had been left behind.

They moved over to the final hut, it was in darkness as all the windows were boarded up. No sound came from inside. They opened the doors slowly, this time it was Taff's turn to look in. Nothing but an old chair, mattress and a stove on the corner. They knew they had found my old accommodation, it smelt rank and they could tell someone had been in there for some time. It was vacant now so they headed back to Denis. Just as they did they heard the door to the occupied hut open. They got straight down and lay still, a man walked over in the direction of them, stopped about two metres off them and started having a piss. He had his back to Taff and Evo. They thought about jumping him, but if it went wrong they had no backup as Denis and the lads had to be about 150 metres away. It would take too long to get to them. After the man finished his piss he turned and headed back to the hut. Evo and Taff returned back to Denis, wishing they had taken him out, it would have been one less for the group.

Ian radioed in to Dunc's team. He needed them to go deeper into the moors.

Dunc was relieved and with his team in suit they wanted to get out there. After gaining the grid reference to their destination, Platty headed to Jock and Glen. Glen collected his trip flares while Jock filled in the shell scrapes. While packing up the last of their equipment Dunc briefed the team.

"We have to head into the moor. We are needed to close in on the doormen. As you know Tony and Wilson have taken out one team, Donny was stabbed, but is stable. Denis Welsh has taken the backup teams and are to hit the huts. We know there is at least two of the doormen there, hopefully he will get some more info about the hunting teams." Dunc handed Platty a piece of paper. "This is the grid we need to get to and we need to be in place by 05:00 hours. We have to try and get between the doormen groups and try to slow them down. We are hoping that it will be the right place. Ian reckons Tony's team is in sight of one group and Ian predicts if we go now we should get there as Tony's team pass them. We need to be ready to support them to take them down."

There was no discussion, they didn't need any more time to question. Platty and Jock looked after the map reading checking the compass every 400 to 600 metres. Dunc kept lead and lookout. Every few metres he checked 360 degrees. Glen held the rear, they walked hard, they kept course, the fight now felt like theirs.

The sound of movement had stopped and the smell of burning had ignited the air. Wilson and Tony kept focused, they each monitored their 180-degree radius keeping Donny as centre point. After five minutes Wilson moved away from the entry point of the woods to Tony. He motioned that he was moving in to take a look.

He stayed low walking heel to toe. He kept watch to the denser concentration of smoke until he found the origin. It was a campfire. Eight men sat around it. They laughed and joked and knocked back drinks. They bragged about previous hunts, and taking pleasure in torturing before executing the men they hunted. They had nailed a man to the ground, legs spread while taking turns to kicking him in the nuts. They had pissed in his mouth and lay their shit on top of him. They had crushed men's skulls and amputated their limbs. Hung men on trees while they butchered his friends in front of him. Every sick bastard tried to out-do the last with tales of horror and then they would laugh. Laugh like their victims were nothing. Laughed like it never haunted them, only made them crave it all to take part again. These savages were not men, they were not even human. They had murdered fathers and sons, brothers and partners and they had been doing it for years.

Wilson's knee rested down slightly, breaking possibly the only dry twig that lay upon the moist spongy ground. His blood chilled as if to mask his body temperature with his surroundings. He didn't like his and Tony's chances against eight men, not with having to defend Donny as well. The groups at the campfire were shushed as they stood to look around. They clung to machetes and axes, shovels and sticks. Some pulled down masks as others removed their coats and shirts revealing their bare chests. They growled and beat chests like Viking warlords. For the first time Bob Wilson felt true fear. It was raw and primal and didn't respect his character. It could make him wretch and groan and slide away from this place. It could make him leave two men behind and never stop running. He fought hard to pull himself back together. He felt his heart beat loud in his ears while his hands and feet seemed miles away from his body. He sunk closer to the ground and kept still.

"We know you're near!" one shouted, circling the men at the fire. "The others used to head here to. Truth is, everyone gets caught in here. Everyone dies in the woods."

24: Damaged

I couldn't settle. I had a bad feeling that something was not right. Kenny and Brit felt the same. We lay behind some shrubs, and tried to listen for any noise... Not a sound. We still felt uneasy, we had been in the woods for about 30 minutes and hadn't seen anyone. Everything was quiet. Strangely quiet. While we still had about an hour's light left, Brit thought we should set up some traps, just in case. Kenny got us to get everything we had hidden on our bodies and lay it all out. I took everything out of my pockets and around my waist. I stood up and as I did a light caught my eye. I got down. Quick!

"Shhhh! There's a light over the top of the bush."

Brit moved to the edge of the wood to have a good look. It was definitely a light, a fire he thought. It looked a good mile away. The light was small and we couldn't smell its smoky breath. It must be the doormen, none of the army lads, if any were out there, would take the risk of being spotted. They had perhaps followed us in here, the decoy hadn't worked. Brit looked at us.

"Look, they are there for the night, they wouldn't take the time to start a fire if they weren't setting up camp for the night. We need to get some traps sorted and get a little rest before first light."

Kenny had already put the items in separate piles and he gave us a pile each.

"Geordie you go to where we came into the wood and make it look like the best way in. Look for a good branch on the tree that has plenty of spring in it."

I knew straight away what he was up to so I got on it. The opening we took refuge in was relatively closed in. Kenny wanted to reduce the entry points to a bottleneck, in case any groups would try to enter. Brit was given the old nails that he had got out of the fire pit back at the hut.

"You need to find a good strong branch and hammer them nails though it. It should make a good club," Kenny told Brit.

We kept it as quiet as possible. Kenny joined me at the front of the wood; the tasks kept our minds busy. Kenny walked out and kept looking back, he seemed to have gone as far as he needed. He lay down and was looking back at the area I was working on, then got up and headed back to me.

"That looks fine mate," he said then handed me a length of rope and asked me to get about seven bits of wood. I passed Brit, he had completed the club, and it looked hellish, like something you'd see in the medieval section of a museum. He gave me a hand with the wood. When we took it back to Kenny he had the piece of metal from the bottom of the chair and a piece of wood about five inches long. He split it down the middle and pushed the metal in and wrapped a piece of cord we'd pulled from the mattress around it. It was a knife. Crude, but deadly and far more effective than the one we'd found in the shed.

I pulled a strong thin branch from a tree and attached several plaited strands from the rope to each end. I got the tension as tight as I could to make a primitive bow. I hadn't shot one in years but I had always been good at it. I gathered some small thin branches, shaved one end into points and the other I made cross splits. I had picked up some feathers throughout the day and with them I made flights. I had made a half dozen arrows and strapped them to my back with my belt. We had luck on our side as the low sun gave us decent light to work and enough shade to remain unnoticed.

As the sun left the sky, the moon swam higher and the light began to grow less workable, so we decided to try and rest. It had to be about 02:00 hours now so I took first watch and got the lads to get their heads down for a while. I knew we wouldn't sleep, but we could at least rest.

Tony lay with Donny. He had managed to pull over some fallen branches and lay them on top of them both. His breathing was slow but his heart was racing. For the last hour he had listened to the sound of Bob Wilson taking the beating of his life. He hadn't screamed, he hadn't shouted. The last words he said to Tony were *"They have found me. There are eight men, stay with Donny. I'm turning my radio off now."* He could have made it back, Tony knew he could but Wilson would have never lead the men back to Tony and Donny. That was the kind of man he was.

It was pitch black now, and all Tony could do now was wait. Wait for first light to come and he was moving in. Wilson could be dead by now but he couldn't live with himself if he didn't try to get him. He didn't close his eyes, not once. He lay on the soft moist ground thinking of every way he was going to take his revenge.

Denis had stormed into the hut with Taff and Evo. The three doormen had been sitting at a table playing cards. They jumped up screaming like scared children. They weren't expecting anyone at the hut for at least another day.

They took one man each and got them on the floor with little effort. Denis Welsh's last man, Grayson stood outside covering the door. They hadn't expected any more company but they knew one rogue hunter was still out there and the huts may be his destination.

Evo grabbed one of the doormen and dragged him to his feet. He edged him over and sat him on one of the chairs, and then Taff tied him to it. They didn't even have to threaten him with another kicking.

"Don't hit me *please don't*, I will tell you anything! *Please don't hurt me!*" he cried.

The lads couldn't believe it. The man was big, bigger than them. You could tell he could handle himself in a fight but here he was, broken and begging like a coward. Evo struck a punch, right on his nose. Blood flowed instantly and he began to scream. It was so loud that Denis gagged him. The other two men just lay there. They never said a word. The look on their faces said it all, they had lost this. The terror on their faces seemed real. However, as Denis stared at them he realised, it was not a fear for his team, but what the packs would do to them when they found out they had lost their base.

Kenny and Brit had nodded off and with a few hours of rest I was starting to feel a bit better. My swelling had gone down a bit, but I could now feel the tender bruising coming out. I lay at the edge of the wood, looking out to the direction we had come. The light off the moon was bright, and lit up the moors beautifully. It was warm with a gentle breeze that cooled my warm skin. I started thinking about times when I had gone camping with friends in my school days. It was just in the local woods, by my parents' house. I was never allowed to venture away from the area I lived, but that night I felt free and at the same time I felt safe. I knew this feeling wouldn't last long, I would have to wake Brit and Kenny up soon and we'd have to set off again. But for now, I wanted to exist in this moment for as long as possible. I never got my wish. In the distance I heard a voice and then there was laughter. Someone was close.

I lifted myself from the ground quietly, and edged to a clearing facing into the wood. The twinkle of the campfire was still present, but now it was joined by three more flames. They moved around the camp like fireflies, swooping to and fro. It took me a moment to realize that they were torches. One in particular raised the hairs on the back of my neck. It shone brighter and grew larger. It was getting closer.

I edged closer to Kenny and Brit and as I did a flock of birds flew overhead, breaking the silence with the flapping of their wings. I used the disturbance to make the noise I needed to get up and squat down closer to my lads. I give them a gentle shove making sure they stayed quiet.

"We have to go now lads," I whispered. I knew we should take the traps down, so we could have the ropes and other items back, in case we needed them later. Just as I went to dismantle the first trap, I looked out of the area, I saw where the torches were coming from, and could see silhouettes in the distance, four men – it was one of the doormen's groups. I swallowed hard but knew we didn't have time. I quickly got back out of sight, and signaled to Kenny and Brit. They came and crouched down beside me. I pointed out towards them. We looked at each other and knew we couldn't get away from this, we would have to stay and fight. It was our best chance, our *only* chance.

We stood together, as we always had. We held tightly to our crude weapons. I started to load my bow, it felt flimsy but I knew its limits. I didn't know how straight it would shoot, but the tension it gave should fire the arrows well enough to do some damage. I looked to Kenny and Brit. My confidence in surviving this plummeted. Brit stood biting his lip and caught me staring at him.

"We've got this Geordie," he said with a split second bloodstained grin. Kenny looked straight ahead, his focus was tight, and I could see by his rapid blinking he couldn't see very well. It was taking everything he had to focus his vision, but this would not stop him.

"You're right Brit," I said. "We've fucking got this."

25: Showdown

The light began to grow in the wood. Tony began to shake his limbs free from atrophy. He was ready to move and find Wilson and the men who had hurt him. He listened for a few minutes in silence before pulling more foliage cover onto Donny. When Donny was covered, Tony began to move forward to Wilson's last heading. In between his footsteps he heard another's.

Tony crouched down slowly and waited. The footsteps were shallow and soft, but there was more than one set. Tony gripped his shovel tightly and over his shoulder ready to swing. His senses were high, he could pinpoint the direction of the footsteps, and took cover around the trunk and high, exposed roots of a large tree stump. He peered through one of the gaps in the rotten roots, and saw four figures enter the tree line. The relief was instant and brought a smile to his face.

"Took you arseholes long enough," he said.

Tony briefed Dunc, Glen, Jock and Platty on the events of the night. They were keen to head straight into the doormen's camp and let loose. But they needed a plan. They decided to go in from four sides. Dunc would take point while Tony would take the rear. Glen and Jock would come from either side, while Platty would stay with Donny. Platty was eager to fight but they couldn't afford for another man to be taken. They needed to get Wilson back, then help me,

Kenny and Brit. Any more rescue missions could put the whole job in jeopardy.

They were ready, and began to move in. Before they parted Tony spoke,

"Don't hold back, they have every intention of making us suffer before finishing us off. These scumbags are out for hell, so *WE* will give them hell."

They had ten minutes to get in position. Dunc was about twenty metres from the camp, only four men remained. Two were slumped down, while two others sat talking. There was no sign of Wilson yet. He gave two fast clicks on his radio. Glen and Jock were next to check in. They gave three clicks. Tony was the last. After his signal all men would move. The two slow clicks went over the radio. The teams went in.

Dunc ran into the camp startling the two lads who were talking at the fire. They stood up fast. One held an oversized machete. It was well worn and looked like it had stories to tell, while the second held a long steel bar. Its end went into a spike and it appeared to be a custom javelin stick.

"You came for what's left of your mate?" the machete owner said. His eyes were large and wide.

The second man nudged the two who lay sleeping.

"Play time, boys," he said.

With that the two other men stood and grabbed their weapons. They started to walk toward Dunc. As they moved closer, Tony and the lads ran straight at them from behind, screaming and shouting.

Jock, swung his mace at the first man he came to. The end of the chain hit him right across the cheek; it split wide open decorating the nearby trees and as he was going down, the shovel from Tony came down on the back of his head.

Glen gripped his dagger and gave three precise jabs to his opponent. He slashed his weapon hand, making the man drop the head of his axe. It spun down striking his knee, while another slash hit his left shoulder making him drop its oversized handle. The last stab tore across both thighs sending the man down to his knees.

Tony smashed the shovel into his next opponent's face. He spun around but did not fall, his momentum swung his studded baseball bat into the shovel's base. The impact took the handle from Tony's hands. He stood unarmed, while the man rushed him with the bat. He was large and clumsy, with his force missing the several swings he took at Tony. As he stepped back, his foot hit one of the rucksacks that lay on the floor, bringing Tony down hard on his back. He turned to pull himself up, and as he did, saw Wilson tied vertically and upside down, to a tree to his right. His hands and feet were tied around the girth of the tree. His bones dislocated or broken to achieve this impossible pose. His mouth was gagged and like his face was blood red.

Dunc was struggling with his fight. He stood against the man with the javelin. He was doing well to defend the strikes toward him with his machete, but the length of his weapon compared to the reach of his opponent, only opened few opportunities to be on the offence. Glen had knocked down his target, and it didn't appear he was getting up anytime soon, so he moved in to help Dunc. He quietly got into place, and was about to make a rush at him, when a sharp pain hit him in the calf. He turned and saw the bloodied face of Jock's target, who had managed to pull himself a few yards across the ground and get one of their smashed beer bottles acquainted with Glen's leg. He spun and returned the favour with his boot to the man's face. He was out again but the weight he put on his injured leg, brought him down on top of the man he just put out.

Jock had swung his mace above his head, and went in to help Tony, who he noticed had just landed on his ass. He came in from the left and swung the mace at the hands of Tony's attacker. The chain snagged one of the bat's studs pulling both weapons from both men. Jock dived in with his fists, bringing the man straight down. He laid into his face and did not stop.

Tony slid over to Wilson, his eyes were bloodshot and surrounded with dried dirt, but they were open.

"Are you ok, Bob?" Tony asked. He knew it was a stupid question. Wilson looked like hell. His body, contorted around the base of the tree for hours, and held upside down would have given him a substantial headache. Tony pulled the gag from Wilson's mouth and looked around for anything to cut him down. He remembered the knife strapped to his hip and took it straight to the rope strapped around Wilson's shoulders. "Hold on Bob, we've left a few of these fuckers for you to finish off."

Dunc was getting nowhere. His efforts were not wearing his opponent down, nor was he stranger with his weapon. He used it well and deflected many of his strikes. He was going to have to grab it, grab it with both hands to get it off him. He was going to have to drop his weapon to do it. He deflected a jab to his chest and managed two slashes with his machete before dropping it and grabbing the steel pole. He had only managed to get grip of the bottom few inches, but didn't have much leverage to wriggle the weapon free. But he clung onto it with everything he had. His opponent then used his strength to push the pole forward, taking Dunc backwards and fast. He stumbled and fell on his back while his attacker slid down the pole on top of him. He lost his grip on the pole, but now, was on top of Dunc at a much better vantage. He immediately grabbed Dunc's throat and piled his 18 stone weight into his arms. Dunc was losing this and couldn't make a sound come from his mouth. His eyes rolled and his body started to convulse, with the lack of oxygen to his lungs.

Suddenly his grip eased. Dunc wretched and coughed, and saw the man was now lifting from his chest. He looked to his side and could see his machete, it dripped with blood and belonged to a new owner. It was now in the hands of Donny.

We stood still in the position we had taken up. I could feel my hands shaking as I held the bow at tension. I fought the urge to ease down; men were coming and they knew we were near.

They chanted the song burned to my memory when they set us off. "RUN, RUN, RUN" and their encores were blood lusting laughter and cheers. Their torchlight grew brighter, with every step forward they took a drum beat which grew louder in my ears. It felt the land below us was the chest of a waking giant, and its exhilarated heartbeats were pulsing through my body. I didn't turn my head to the others, I knew they would feel the same. We kept focus to the entry way, hoping this would be our greeting point.

They approached the entrance. They stopped and looked in. Darkness kept us hidden but we prayed that there was nothing to see, prayed we hadn't left anything obvious on show. Two of them started to enter.

I got my first glimpse, it was them from the club. 'The prat' was with them, Big Bob, Steve and one more, I couldn't work out. Steve and the unknown man were shirtless, their skin decorated with dried blood that was not their own. I prayed it wasn't Donny's.

Big Bob and Steve came in first. Slowly they approached, their heavy breaths melted the slight morning chill releasing a fine vapour. I held my breath not wanting to alert them with mine. 'The prat' and the other man stayed out until Steve and Big Bob had got inside. Just as 'the prat' started to move he touched one of Kenny's traps.

Kenny had loaded a few branches with nails and loaded them with springs we took from the chair back at our shed. He wedged them just right in some uneven ground; if their counterweight was disturbed, the springs would release. It worked. Up came the trap. It flew with such high velocity, it embedded into Big Bob's face. He fell to the floor in a howl of agony. A few stray nails had caught Steve on the torso, which sent him back over; he was on the ground, rolling around in pain. Big Bob pulled at the wood at his face. None of the nails were straight, they pulled and ripped his flesh with any movement – for now he was occupied.

Brit and Kenny ran straight at 'the prat' and the unknown man. They ran past Steve. I aimed my arrow at him and let it fly. It flew straight past him so I loaded another. By this time, he had got to his feet and began to come towards me. I let out another arrow, it landed in his chest. He went back a step then looked down, pulled the arrow that had burrowed an inch into his skin. It spat a geyser of blood as it withdrew. I had another loaded, as he began to charge at me. His eyes bulging and mouth growling, like the rabid dog he was. I exhaled as I set the arrow away. It hit his left eye. This time embedded around three inches. He fell straight back down to the ground. I had killed him. This bothered me, I knew this was a life or death situation, but it still didn't seem right. We were not in an army situation and we could end up in prison. But it was him or me. For now, that's all that mattered.

Kenny jumped at the one we didn't have a name for. The hand-made knife was lunged straight into the side of his neck. It sliced straight though his jugular vein, not a sound escaped his wide-open mouth. His hand came up to the knife, and his eyes looked into Kenny's and seemed to stay for an eternity. He took a long loud gasp of air, as if he had got his strength back and was going to lift Kenny off his feet with one swipe of his strong hand. Instead, he sank to his knees and fell forward onto his face.

Brit went straight for 'the prat'. He swung the club at him. The only defence 'the prat' could muster was to lift his pathetic arms to protect his face. The nails sank deep into the skin. The heavy swing caused Brit to lose balance. He stumbled over an old fallen tree branch with his hand slipping his grasp on the club. As he did I had an arrow back in the bow and let it fly; it missed the target, flashing past Kenny. Prat pulled the club out of his arm, then swung for Brit. With it he turned to get up. Brit screamed out, the bat was stuck to his back. 'The prat' turned as if to gain praise for taking a man down, but saw his team were gone. Only Big Bob was moving, trying to ease the studded branch from his face with difficulty. Pete did exactly what we expected him to do. He ran.

I loaded the bow once more, this time I took aim and it sank into the back of this thigh. He fell to the ground, mid sprint, which sent him into a roll. Kenny ran up to him holding his makeshift blade. I knew the next few moments would change his life forever. Revenge he deserved, and the truth was I'd fantasised so many times about ending the little rat, but the difference between us and them is that killing for the sake of killing would change us. When the adrenalin, the anger and absolute exhaustion we all had wore off, nothing good comes from killing like this – what would be left? It would pray on our waking thoughts and haunt our dreams.

"KENNY, STOP!" I shouted.

He turned and looked at me in bewilderment. Then looked back at the man laying at his feet. I knew he recognised that he was the one we had named 'the prat'. He knew I told him he was mine. I headed toward Kenny, helping Brit to his feet as I passed. Blood was seeping through his shirt in several places. He winced with nearly every step as the tender, mangled flesh touched his clothing. Kenny stood over Pete, still struggling to catch his breath. He stared into Pete's face as Pete did the same. He looked weak and remorseful; this made me hate him even more. As Brit reached the fallen Prat, he moved down close to him and grabbed the arrow which still perturbed his thigh. He grabbed and twisted it. Pete howled in pain.

"Brit, that's *enough*," I said while looking at Pete.

Brit stood up and looked at me with a million questions in his eyes, but he never spoke. Kenny on the other hand, didn't yet understand my reservation.

"Do it Geordie, *KILL THAT PIECE OF SHIT!*" he said.

I never took my eyes from Pete; his now were bright red and tearing up.

"Please don't kill me, *please*. Let me go and I'll lead the other teams away from you ... you can get away," said 'the prat'. His voice was much higher pitched and pathetic.

I had no intention of letting him go, but I had forgotten for a moment that other teams were out there; they could be close so we had to get on the move again. I did what I had to. I took Kenny's blade and lunged it once, twice, three times into Pete's opposite thigh before I had to take back control of my hand again. It wanted to continue to silence this scumbag, but I couldn't let myself become that man, ever. The man that enjoyed to kill. He screamed out, and I felt nothing. I tore a length of denim from his trousers that Kenny's blade had assisted with and tied it over his mouth. I stood and walked back towards the area we had set our traps. I stopped in my tracks when I noticed a few packs dropped around the outside of our entrance. They must have taken them off when the fight began. I motioned to Kenny and Brit who instantly moved down to take a look. They searched the bags and found a day's worth of food, torches, knives, cable ties, lighters and water.

We started on the water, downing as much as we could. None of us had even realized we hadn't drank all day. I left the lads to make a dent on the rations while I moved back over to Peter. I grabbed his feet, and pulled him over to our temporary camp. I frisked him down and cable tied his feet and hands. I moved over to Steve and pulled his lifeless body over to Pete. Sweat was starting to collect on my face and Brit joined me when he saw me wiping it from my face.

"Go get a quick bite Geordie I'll get—" Brit stopped mid flow. "Fuck lads, Big Bob."

I turned and found the spot where he had fallen.

Big Bob was gone.

26: The Road Runner

Evo was only getting pleas from the coward he had in the chair. He smacked him hard after every question. Denis' eyes rolled. He was done with this one. He looked down to the other two men on the floor. One was looking straight at the ground where a pool of tears and snot had gathered while the other was staring straight at him.

"What you looking at prick?" Denis asked.

The man glanced over to a large black box sat on the centre desk, then straight back to Denis. He moved down close to the man, and before he got the chance to speak the man whispered in his ear.

"Take me alone, and I'll tell you everything."

Denis walked over to the table, picked up the box that sat in the middle. It was a lockable document box, the ones intended for important papers that could withstand a fire, while keeping its contents unharmed. He tried to open it but it was unsurprisingly locked. He tucked it under his arm and paced the room, while Evo continued to get nothing but cries and begging from his man. That was enough, Ian had asked them to gather any helpful intelligence they could, but this was taking too much time. His men were out there, and they needed them. Denis put his hand on Evo's shoulder.

"Get me that one," he said pointing at the man on the ground, staring at them. "And strap up his hands and feet. I'm taking him to the next hut."

Denis dragged the man with Grayson, to the hut with all the cars stored. He got Evo and Taff to keep an eye on the two men he left behind and to check for any keys for the vehicles.

The cars and vans were tightly parked. At least twelve cars and two vans were stored. Within the entryway there was also some old farming equipment. They were rusted and covered in webs. Denis pulled his man over to what looked like an old tractor bucket.

"OK then," said Denis "Tell me everything."

He waited in the car. The bag was in the glove box, as promised. Every hour he stepped out to listen for his rendezvous and have a smoke, to calm his nerves. He'd waited three hours around this vehicle, one of them was time overdue. He'd have to accept that certain eventualities had occurred and that he may have to move on to plan B. This worried him. If he left his man out here, there would be consequences. Worse than those fates of the men who'd died in the moors. Betrayal of the 'Alpha Wolf' was a public death, but this didn't come quick. It lasted days.

"Why are you betraying your mates then? No honour in that. I thought you scumbags would stick together." Denis said to the man sat before him. The man stared at the ground, as if finding a place to start his story. Denis didn't care for any sob story he got back, he just wanted anything that could help. The man lifted his head and then slowly opened his eyes.

"They are not my mates. They have not one shred of honour between them. What I'm going to tell you will end me. So, you'll have to forgive my apprehension."

Denis swallowed. He felt slightly unnerved by what was

to come. "Go on," he said, less urgently than his previous tone.

"This isn't about the army, it isn't about any prejudices. It's about money, and it's way bigger than you could ever imagine. Whatever you do here today, rescue your men, take down this hunt, it's nothing. These things go on everywhere and the men that organise these hunts are untouchable." The man paused to lick his lips and take a look at the doorway. "Big Bob found most of his help on the streets. He'd give us food and shelter if we did things for him … terrible things."

"What kind of things?" asked Denis.

"We were the baiters, we'd find the men, too drunk to put up a fight, or ones who were alone. We'd start up a fight with them, so the doormen could intervene and take them outside. The people in the club wouldn't think anything of it, just taking out the rubbish, but they'd get them in their vans. The packs operate in clubs all over the country. They have done this hundreds of times. They charge the men to take part in the hunt. Depending on the *livestock* they call it, It's five hundred to a grand per entry, plus any side bets they put on. That tin you're holding has this hunt's winnings in."

Denis looked down to the tin he held in his arms; just holding it he felt like some kind of accessory to the atrocity. Blood money, death money, whatever it was, it showed the true value of Geordie and the lads. Denis knew as well as anyone the drive men have for money. And felt a new sense of urgency to get out to the moors.

The sun was now getting high, he couldn't rely on the veil of darkness of hiding his exit. The window of the car was down, and the cool breeze flooded in. He checked his watch, 07:14. He bit his lip and looked anxiously out to the woods.

A sound stole his attention. It was movement and it was coming fast. He took grip of his pistol and held it just out of view from the window. A single figure had become apparent inbetween the bushes about twenty metres from the car, it was one the man was familiar with.

"Jesus Bob, you look like shit," he said as he stepped out of the car.

"Fuck you Mick!" said Big Bob.

"What happened to your face Bob?" Mick asked.

Bob's face was bleeding from a collection of around twenty small holes.

"I was hit by an army boy trap. But it doesn't matter now. We have to get moving, there are more army boys out here. I think they've already took down one of the packs—"

"*Two* packs Bob," Mick interrupted "Mine got hit last night, they got Ray and Dave."

Bob rubbed his sweating head.

"Well, bigger share for us then, Mick." Bob laughed as he tried to open the passenger car door. "Well open the fucking thing, Mick, so we can get the fuck out of here!" Bob turned to see Mick with a pistol aimed at his face.

"Why are you telling me this? You know you'll be going to prison for this? I'm no way in hell letting you go, for telling your sob story!" Denis was angry. He couldn't tell if the man was just killing time or playing to get favour for him.

"I'm telling you this because I can't do this anymore. The stakes are getting higher as the demand is getting bigger, and I want no more part in it. If the Alphas can make money from perversions like this, then they will, and what after? Men who want to hunt women? Kids? If people will pay, these fuckers will make it happen." The man looked back to the doorway and over to Denis. "The keys to all the cars are in the red wall locker over there." He motioned his head to the rear wall on the right.

Denis looked at Grayson and nodded for him to go check it out.

"They knew you might be coming out here, well, Big Bob and Mick anyway. I heard them planning a worst-case scenario."

Denis' stomach turned over but he didn't let it show, he coughed. "How would they know?"

"Mick suspected Donny, he recognised him from the club the night your men were taken. I did too because I was there." The man gulped like he was holding back the urge to vomit. "I baited your lads that night," said the man, his eyes burning red with the release of a single tear. He was just a kid, no more than nineteen years old, but Denis' fury sent a strong right hook to his face.

"What the fuck are you doing?" Big Bob stared at Mick. His face looked calm and it worried him.

"So, you know what I think Bob? I think you should have listened to me. I told you that we may have a mess out here, yet your greed got in the way. You know what happens if we get exposed. The Circle gets exposed and you know what those guys would do to us?" Mick waited briefly for an answer. Bob hesitated.

"Stop fucking around Mick, you couldn't do this to me! Are you stupid? You know who my allies are and if they find out they will be finding pieces of you for weeks!"

Mick smiled, "Well that's just it Bob, *I* didn't do this to you, the army boys did. You got injured, made a run for it, then you got caught. Your team will tell everyone you got away. I walk out as a victim, a victim of *your* fuck up. Now turn around and put your hands behind your head."

Big Bob turned and put up his hands.

"They'll know it wasn't those lads that got me, they don't have guns. Now stop fucking around, take the money if that's what you need and we'll speak nothing more about this."

"Bob, Bob, Bob, how stupid do you think I am? And what makes you think I'm going to shoot you?" Mick tried to take Big Bob in a choke hold. Bob turned quickly and reversed the hold onto Mick, while stamping on the back of his knee. Mick's neck cracked hard as the weight of his body took a sharp fall. Bob held on tight until his convulsing stopped.

Denis stood there panting hard. He'd hit the man over and over till his fists were numb. The man spat blood onto the ground but made no attempt to defend himself or beg Denis to stop.

"I'm not asking you to let me go, but I won't go to prison. They'll find me wherever I am when they find out I've spoken with you."

Denis didn't need to know anything else. He needed a moment to think. He stepped to the rear of the hut where Grayson was. "Find anything?" he asked.

"They are all here, keys with the vehicle registrations on their chains and this one I think is for your box." Grayson handed Denis a small silver key with a large unmarked key chain on. Denis looked over to the man sat across the room and felt guilt over splitting his face. This man, this *boy* was doing things for a bigger power; he acted like he had no choice. Maybe for him there was none but he had been brave enough to own up to it. More than what a lot of people in his position would ever do. Denis started to walk back over to him, when he noticed he started to rock back and forth on the chair.

"My name is Billy by the way. Tell your friends I'm sorry."

His momentum took him backwards with enough force to embed one of the rusted tractor bucket teeth through his skull. His eyes remained open, his mouth now closed forever.

Bob rolled Mick's body over to the bushes he emerged through a few minutes earlier. He used a large fallen branch with leaves to dust away the prints between his resting place and the car. He started the car and drove slow for the first few miles through the rough ground. He never looked back. He left the moors behind. He left Mick behind and headed south.

Denis lay Billy's body inside the tractor bucket. He covered it with a piece of waterproof tarp that lay over one of the cars. He bound the other two men together and lay them on the stinking mattresses in the prison shed. They took the keys to a silver Land Rover and carefully reversed it out of the hut. They had contacted Ian with an update, and had their mission. They headed north.

As the car got underway Denis sat in the back seat holding the key to the black tin box which sat next to him. *Fuck it*, he thought and opened the box. Inside were four heavily stained volumes of an old children's book. They were dirty and bloated from years of going damp and drying out. Probably from one of the old huts they just departed from. "What the hell?" said Denis as he took out the books. Only one book still had its cover and the faded words could only just be made out: *The Road Runner*.

He pulled over for a moment. His body sweating, his head spinning. Mick opened the glove box and took out the brown hessian bag. It stank of root vegetables making him wretch. He put his hand inside and pulled out a tight neat bundle. He counted fifty wrapped bundles each containing a grand. His head was clearer now, his sweating stopped. Mick started the car up again and rejoined the road.

27: Fractured

Tony had got Wilson down from the tree. He grimaced in pain as his limp body fell back down to the ground. His shoulders were unevenly set back. He had spent enough time in the base's gym to recognise a dislocation. He put Wilson's hand to his shoulder and put his hand on his elbow. With his other, he guided Wilson's shoulder and with a quick jerk, he popped the arm back into his socket. He jumped over Wilson's body and repeated to his right side. Within minutes his fingers started to move again and his crimson face had settled to look more human.

Platty helped Jock with his injured calf. He removed a few fragments of glass from the wound and got it bandaged up. Dunc and Glen took care of the clean-up. They tied up and gagged all the bodies, dead or alive, and threw them on top of each other. Dunc marked the location on his map.

Donny walked over to Tony and Wilson.

"Fun exercise this turned out to be eh Bob?"

Bob laughed but immediately regretted it when he grabbed his ribs in pain.

"Glad to have you back Donahue. You ready to come get the rest of these bastards?" Wilson asked.

Donny blinked and looked at his B.S.M. He looked just how Donny felt, but his spirit remained gleaming. He said the only thing he could say, the only thing he wanted to say,

"Yes, Sir."

Tony radioed into Ian, filled him in on all that had gone down. He relayed the coordinates of the teams they had taken down. Ian had also just been updated on Denis' team and would pass on the coordinates, so he could pick up all the fallen men.

Ian had compiled a head count. From the twenty-two men, nine had been apprehended and thirteen were still at large. They hadn't discovered the three we had taken down, that left ten. Ten men against our seventeen. The odds were moving in our favour.

Donny felt alright considering. His wound felt tight and had started to mesh. His movements felt restricted and he still had a pounding head, but he felt ready to get back on with the mission. Wilson still looked like shit. His face showed his body was in pain and his coat stank of piss – his captors obviously used his body as their urinal overnight. He didn't remove it. Donny couldn't tell if it was hiding any hidden injuries or if it was keeping his body together but for the moment he spoke strong, and didn't show any signs of weakness.

The team sat for a while plotting out their next move. Tony and Donny thought it best if the team split up to cover more ground. This time Tony would head out with Wilson, Jock and Platty. Donny with Dunc and Glen.

They headed deeper into the moors. Dunc set his course for north west while Tony north easterly. Both teams kept going until about 12:00pm, only stopping for a quick check of the map and compass and for the odd piss.

I noticed Brit nursing his back, I knew he'd never complain about it, so I made an excuse to stop for a moment to catch my breath.

"How's your back mate?"

"It feels like shit."

I knew he must be feeling pretty bad for Brit to admit to any weakness. This was his style. I often thought Brit wouldn't complain even if his head was on fire. He'd just take it and deal with it. In this case, it was more than pride, Brit kept his shit together for us.

"Let me take a quick look over it." I rolled up his shirt and saw the raw dotted flesh that 'the prat' had inflicted. I ripped a length of fabric from his frayed shirt along its hemline, pouring some of the water down his back and over the fabric. I wiped as much of the stray dirt and blood away and it didn't look too bad. We had nothing clean left to bandage up his wound so I rolled his shirt back down.

"You still crying about that, you soft cockney!" Kenny said.

Brit smiled. "Up yours, you monkey hanging twat!" It was good to hear they still had good banter with one another.

It had to be about 15:00. hours when Dunc's team spotted a group way ahead of them. It would take several hours to catch up to them. Donny got on the radio to Tony; whilst he did Glen and Dunc were trying to work out a way to catch up to them quicker. Glen thought, if he could run off ahead and call out to the doormen's group they may head towards him. Trouble, Dunc didn't agree, it was dangerous, he didn't want to take the chance on anyone else getting caught. Tony's team had made good ground and was in a better location to close in. If Dunc's team could just keep on their tail, reporting back to Tony with their location, Tony could try to work out the point where they could make an ambush.

I couldn't stop thinking about what I had done. I'd killed Steve and possibly left Pete to bleed out. In the Falklands I was a gunner. I lay down cover fire for troops on the front line. I never knew if any bullets I fired had killed a man. It was a high possibility but I never saw their faces, I didn't know their names so the reality of it never prayed on my thoughts. All that kept playing in my mind, was my crude excuse for an arrow embedded in Steve's eye. It was the look on his face. The moment his life was extinguished. I knew at the time it was either him or me and there wasn't an option to do any negotiation. It was life or death. It wasn't just the killing that got to me but the fact that we could end up in big trouble over the whole situation. This was not war and the law would play a part in all this if we made it out. It would look at both sides of this. I could only imagine the stories that would come from the doormen.

My thoughts were suddenly halted when Kenny stopped walking, he wanted a rest. I'd seen him stumble quite a bit, nearly falling over but like the rest of us, he was exhausted. Me and Brit took time to search the landscape. There was no one. We took off our packs to see if there was anything left to eat. Our water was running low. We'd have to start looking for any streams to restock. The rubbing from Brit's pack had left his shirt saturated with blood. I took all his items out and put them in mine while Kenny rolled up the empty rucksack in case any of its parts could help us out. It's one rule you never forget in survival training. Everything can be useful.

The sun was up high and the warm air breeze gently brushed against my face. I closed my eyes and felt so relaxed that I could have dropped off to sleep. But the image came back to me, Steve's last face, sleep was not going to happen.

After around half an hour Kenny gave me a kick in the leg. "Come on Geordie, we had better be off." I didn't understand why but I felt overcome with anger and bit at Kenny.

"Off to *where*, Kenny? Do any of us know where the fuck we are heading? We've been walking the Mowers all day."

I knew we had to move, I knew movement meant survival, but the words escaped my mouth without my control. I saw Kenny's face turn red, he was shouting at me. His hands were up in the air, but I didn't hear a word he said. My eyes went past him, past Brit moving in to calm him down. They looked into the woods. Something had caught my eye. It was subtle but I could make out. It was a pattern or shapes on the tree. They were not natural, these were made by hands. Some fresher than others. I got up and walked over to it.

The markings were made with crimson spray paint and were around seven feet up the trunk of the tree. I wasn't any good at school, my dyslexia had sorted that out for me but I recognised one of the shapes. It was like a hieroglyph or ancient marking. I had seen it somewhere before. I looked over to the lads who were both staring at me.

"Get over here and look at this."

Kenny and Brit both looked up at the marking.

"I can't see anything Geordie. Stop wasting time and let's move." I could tell Kenny wasn't bothered by this.

"How can you not see that symbol Kenny?" I was frustrated and had a feeling this meant something.

"I can't see much Geordie, I'm… it's my… my… eyes. I'm losing my sight." Kenny looked like he was about to burst into tears, but he quickly wiped his nose on his sleeve and pulled himself together.

"Since the shed, I've been losing my sight and…" he paused wiping his nose again, "…and I don't know how much longer I'll be able to help you."

I felt like an arsehole. I did what I knew Kenny would have hated, I put my arms around him. It only lasted a moment, but it said more than words ever could.

"I'm going to get you out Kenny, you have my fucking word." He patted me hard on the back. Kenny hated weakness, especially on him. I just needed a moment to work this out. Brit was looking up at the tree.

"I saw one like that earlier but thought it was just one of the markings they put on trees they want to cut down." It was a sensible assumption, but it didn't make sense. Who would give a shit about cutting down trees out here in the middle of nowhere? Another symbol was on a tree two over from us. Similar but with different strokes.

"What do they look like? I'm smarter than you two put together so maybe you could describe them," Kenny said with a smirk.

"It's like a horseshoe, but with the capital A over the top of it. Under it there are three teardrop-like shapes and above there are four letters that don't make any sense." Saying what I saw out loud made me feel ridiculous, but it seemed important.

"The horseshoe shape is Omega, it's the last letter of the Greek alphabet. A is Alpha, the first." Kenny paused a moment, like he was putting pieces together. "Brit, where did you see the other markings?"

"I noticed some near the camp we made and then some about an hour away, but don't ask me to remember what those symbols were."

Kenny rubbed his chin and took another moment.

"In the shed we heard 'the prat' talk about the packs, like wolf packs, when he talked about the doormen. In groups of wolves or other predators there are alphas, the leaders. Omegas are maybe the followers?"

It made sense, it couldn't just be coincidence. But what does the rest me an? Brit looked at the shapes, I could tell he didn't get it, but something stood out to him.

"In London some of the gangs would get tear tattoos inked if they took a life. It was a message to anyone they faced that they meant business. You don't think this is the same, do you?"

It was just a guess but it was enough to convince me that these had something to do with the hunt. If so, we had seen at least four to five sets of these in the woods. I suddenly felt like we were being watched and took a minute to take a good look around the horizon around us. Men have been caught in here, and a lot. I began to feel very naïve. We had come to the woods for shelter and refuge, somewhere to hide. It was obvious that is what most men would do and this is where they had been found and killed. We had to leave, it wasn't safe here. I could bet on all the groups heading here. They didn't need to rush as they know where they'd find us.

We moved out, we didn't know where to but we all felt sure the woods was the hunters' playground. They probably knew the area very well and knew they would find us here. We kept going till the sun had started to go down and the tree line was far out of sight. Tonight, we would sleep in the open with nothing but ourselves to hide behind. We were cold, exposed and beyond vulnerable. The day was coming to an end and we continued our desperate search for somewhere to camp for the night. We had nothing to camouflage ourselves with or anything to make traps with. We still had the makeshift knife, club and my bow with five arrows left. We continued to move, looking for dips in the land so we could at least be out of sight.

I kept a close eye on the woodland that lay behind us. Its darkness contrasted with the damp land around it. Death lay in those trunks and it gave me chills thinking of the horrors it had witnessed. Looking back over the moor, the landscape had its ups and downs. We had been careless up till now; we could have missed anyone hiding in the gullies. I decided we should stop at the next high point. We would keep a solid watch for about thirty minutes for any movement.

We settled low on top of the highest verge we could find. It gave us a decent vista of the landscape around us. We took off the backpacks and Brit went through them. He got out all the food items and lay them before us. There was plenty of chocolate, crisps and sugary sweets. He passed the sweets and we sat in silence letting the sugar stimulate our bodies. The sky was welcoming and clear and it took pleasure in stealing my attention. I positioned myself behind Brit to keep our watchtower at its full potential. There was still no movement out there but the night was getting cooler, more so than our previous nights. And as our brief sugar stimulation started to crash I thought we'd need to keep ourselves alert. I started conversation about everything and nothing. It was hard to maintain, until Brit asked Kenny why he had joined the army.

"It was more to get away from the police, I was a bit of a tearaway, always fighting. One day I picked on the wrong lad, it turned out he was a boxing coach. He put me on my

backside but he liked what he saw. He got me into boxing."
Kenny smiled as I recalling a better time in his life. "That
was when I turned it around and thought about the army."
Kenny turned to Brit. We had never heard Brit's story, not
the real one anyway. We had heard rumours, but it had been
a subject of taboo. We knew he'd tell us one day and didn't
expect this night to be any different. Kenny returned his
sights back to his patch of land.

"It was pretty much the same for me, but I was in a gang.
I had started with knives and pretty soon after I got into
guns, I left school and had no job prospects so I did what I
thought would pay my way. it was a policeman that got me
out of it. I was proving myself in some turf war bullshit. I
had to sit at the end of Old Kent Road and to stay there until
Barry Cook came out of his estate. He was another gang
leader. They sent me to kill him. I was just a kid and they
sent me out to murder a lad." Brit paused a moment. We sat
in silence. His memory we guessed he wasn't proud of. "Just
before he came out that policeman came around the corner.
He knew I was in the wrong area and got me in the car. He
could have searched me but I think he knew I was armed.
He drove me back to my estate and on the way lectured me
on prison and what you go though in there. I remember
thinking that I wasn't going there for another man's dispute.
As I got out of the car he said, you should look at the army
son. That's where you get the chance to fight probably in a
fight that means something."

Silence reigned our watchtower again. We all had different
journeys but our reasons had been the same. We wanted a
better life for ourselves. Earn a sense of belonging and a
reason to go forward.

Just as the sun went right down, I changed places with Brit and sat down with Kenny. The cold night air was coming over me. The grass felt damp and I started to shiver. Kenny took off his jacket and put it over my shoulders; it was too small for me but it felt good, still warm from his body heat. I started to nod off when Brit nudged us awake.

"I can see them coming over the small hill in the distance."

He was right. We saw four silhouettes move across the moonlight. We moved down onto our bellies, the damp grass instantly soaked into our shirts. They were headed to the woods. I felt the urge to get moving again but I fought it off. We kept watch till the figures were absorbed into the darkness.

It was a hard decision, the moon wasn't bright enough to follow, but we decided to take a chance and move off. Any more groups passing through to get to the woods may stumble across us. Our chances were only slightly better moving off, being packed up and ready with our weapons made sense. Just before we did I thought if the army is out there looking for us, we should set a trail that they could follow. Something that a civilian wouldn't recognise, or look for. I grabbed a crisp packet and filled it with soil. I got the makeshift knife and chopped the grass around the area and made a small hole. I stuffed the crisp packet into it and lay a tuft of grass over it, just enough so it could still be seen. I scratched out an arrow pointing south. We had a method in our regiment, if we left a clue like this it meant we were heading west, we'd adjust our bearing by one vector in a clockwise direction.

We headed off. I wasn't happy about moving in the dark without map and compass, let alone the ability to use a torch safely but I knew we had no choice. We were so beyond exhausted, that we were forgetting basic training of survival, aviation as well as leaving trails for your comrades to find. I had set our first clue. With any luck our lads would find it.

28: The Omegas

Dunc, Donny and Glen had closed the gap on the doormen. By the end of daylight, they should be within a mile of them. They had agreed with Tony that they should wait until the night fell before making their move. They were ready for their attack. The doormen had made camp and had settled.

Tony and Dunc both had eye contact with the same doormen's group. They didn't seem to be stopping, they walked in a single file, through the woods. Dunc contacted Tony on the radio, if the doormen were not going to stop, they would have to ambush them now. They would get into a horseshoe shape around them, starting with a 75-metre radius to close in on them.

They started to break off to get into position. Tony remained with Wilson, while Jock and Platty split up to meet Donny and Dunc at either side, and Glen took the apex. The group of doormen stopped but they did not sit or move out of their line.

They were ready in position and the lads started to tighten the gap to the doorman group. Still the men had not moved, they stood still in a line. Wilson checked again the group with his binoculars. Something wasn't right. The men were just standing there, their heads aimed down to their chests. He grabbed Tony's arm and shook his head; he handed him the binoculars for Tony to look. But it was too late, the ambush had begun – but not the one that they had planned.

"You ready Dunc?" Platty edged forward, his machete ready for action. They crept forward to a small bush only ten metres away from the doormen group.

"What the fuck are they doing?" Dunc was confused.

Something was not right. The men just stood there like their batteries had worn out. No weapons out and standing in a vulnerable pose. They all faced the same way but eyes to the ground. He looked to Platty and motioned for them to move around a little further, to get a better look. But it didn't matter anymore, into view of the group Jock and Donny had appeared, ready to fight. They were right in front of the doormen group but still they did not move.

Donny and Jock were ready, their hands tightly gripped their weapons. Donny held up his left hand, counting down to rush them. They moved in but didn't get any reaction from the men. They stood hanging with their weapons in the air, but no one moved. Donny approached the men slowly. The light was limited so he had to get close. He approached the first in the line, a hood was over his head. He raised his machete and pulled back the hood. This wasn't one of the hunters. He knew the man's face. It was gagged and his hands tied. Something was gripped in his hands. When Donny moved closer to examine it the gagged man whimpered and shook his head, making a string visible which hung from his nose. It was a grenade. The pin tied with string at one end, and through the man's nose at the other. Donny spun around to Jock. A man stood with him wearing a matching army attire. But he wasn't army and he had a knife to his throat.

"*THE BACKUP TEAM HAVE BEEN COMPROMISED!!*" Donny called but no one came.

Ian's second team had been caught. Their captors had stripped them of their camouflage gear, supplies and radios and dressed them in theirs. Who knows how long ago. They would have heard every last communication to Ian and knew where they were headed.

Snapping twigs came from all around him. Donny stood alone as he saw Tony and Wilson being led out by two men, then Dunc and Platty by two more.

"Well, well. Looks like you squaddie pricks aren't so clever after all."

Ian had contacted his brother Robert. The mission had built up a few more prisoners to bring in, he needed something large to contain them and get them out of the moors. He was satisfied with progress so far. Donny and Wilson had been through what he dreaded, but no major casualties and it looked like things were hopefully starting to wrap up. He hadn't left the pressure cooker for two days and the cabin fever was starting to get to him. Gary Pipes had brought him supplies and a mattress which so far still stood upright in the corner of the room. With Donny back with the teams there was little point him staying put so he needed to get out there. He started to pack up the maps and gear he'd left out over the last few days when he heard something. It was the radio. Three signals, like morse code. He heard it again. The radio was on channel eight. Ian turned the frequency to band three, there was nothing. He turned his back to eight and waited. Three dashes went off again. He turned it to frequency six, the regiment used a clockwise clockface code for any decoy transmissions. He waited a moment and then heard a voice.

"Ian, come in. It's Glen."

"Go ahead Glen."

The radio remained silent for a few minutes. The low sound of Glen's voice suggested he was in trouble. Ian fought the urge to repeat in case Glen was waiting for an opportunity to speak again.

"Backup team two have been caught. They have a radio. They've heard everything."

29: Cold Front

"Come on lads we have to keep going." Brit walked ahead, scouting the land before us. We travelled slow as the weather was changing. The warm days and cool nights had supported us so far, but new cold fronts moved in. The rain had started coming down hard and with a strong wind as backup. We were out in the open and we were getting hammered. The bitter wind battered our faces and the rain seeped into every abrasion on our skin. It felt like tiny shards of glass piercing our flesh. Our clothes were wet through, and our unsuitable loafers were waterlogged. Things were indeed quite shit.

Brit noticed the gap between him and us was opening, we couldn't go on anymore, we had to stop. We regretted taking some of the overcoats from the men we left behind, but we had walked for hours and going back now wasn't an option.

We got down behind a shallow dip in the ground. It shielded us a little from the wind but not the rain, it just seemed to get heavier and our trench began to evolve into a stream. We cuddled up to one another to try and keep warm but Kenny had started shivering really bad. At the moment we couldn't do anything for him. We tried to get him under me and Brit, just to keep him slightly more sheltered. We just had to hang on through this night hoping the morning would bring back the sun.

Glen sunk into the ground. He hadn't been spotted but he watched as his team were thrown to the ground by the doormen. They had caught the standby team that Ian had sent to look for Mick and now they stood in their uniforms and packs. The four man backup team had been clothed in the doormen's attire as a trick to distract our lads from seeing them, as they could sneak up from behind. He wanted to run in to aid his friends but knew he wouldn't make much of a dent in their five-man team. He had contacted Ian and he prayed he could make it through to Denis, in order for them to swiftly get backup. But for now, it was only Glen.

Tony was thrown to the ground, his face dropped into the soft moss of the woodlands floor. He raised it to see Wilson, Donny, Dunc, Jock and Platty in the same predicament. He looked up to the men that stood before him. They were the backup team sent to locate Mick, the rogue hunter. They stood in limbo, their faces freshly battered and bruised. Their feet were tied to the man behind, while hands bound before them, each holding a grenade which was securely taped and detonator pin held in place by the string attached through each man's bloody nose. They couldn't move their heads. If the pin jerked by any sudden movements the detonation would run down the line like falling dominos. Tony couldn't see Glen, he assumed they hadn't found him yet.

The doormen stood behind the two rows of men. They spoke low, with the falling rain and winds creaking the brittle branches it was difficult to hear any words. He did hear the radio, it signaled three times. The men stopped talking and took it out. It signaled again three times. It was Glen, it must be. Tony hoped he had a plan to contact Denis' team. They would be close and hopefully offer the backup the lads clearly needed.

"WE KNOW YOU'RE OUT THERE YOU LITTLE FUCKER," the

doorman snarled. "WE'LL FIND YOU SOON AND HANG YOU WITH THE REST OF YOUR FUCKING MATES!"

Two of the doormen wandered away from the group. They must know Glen is still out there. Three men remained, they began going up the row tying the team's hands behind their heads. Tony was at the end. He knew he'd have to act now, or he'd never get another chance.

Glen rolled across the ground until he hit the base of a tree, he curved his body around it and used the trunk to hide his body. Behind the tree where he stood, was a small verge which had started to fill with water. He removed his pack and took the roll of string he had used for his silent alarm. He tied it low to the trunk then slid down the verge and moved across to the next trunk tying the other end. He had two spare knives, one tucked into the bottle compartment on his bag, the other attached to his ankle strap. He stuck them into the ground on the other side of the verge, blade side up. He slid his poncho from its cover and lay it over the blades, it had a camouflage print and with the darkness it concealed the blades. In his front pack pocket, he had six ninja stars, he took them out and put them in his right jacket pocket. He looked up from the verge and saw about ten metres away the two doormen, they were bearing left from Glen and he needed them to head straight. He took out his torch and aimed it in the space he wanted the men to come. They spotted the light and made a run toward it. Glen threw the torch down between the two trees and got to the other side of the verge. They spotted him. Glen moved backwards, he clung at his leg to imply it was hurt and backed away while facing the men.

"Where do you think you're going, sweetheart?" the men

jeered, moving forward towards the two trees. Glen needed them to run so he turned to make a getaway.

He heard the men fall, they had hit his trip wire. He ran back to the verge to see a face start to emerge. Glen kicked it with every bit of hate he felt. The face disappeared. He moved to the edge of the verge and saw a blade had gone through the other man's abdomen, he clung to it but this wasn't going to stop him. He started to make a run up the verge. Glen kicked him back down, the man spun and landed face first in the small stream that had started to swell. He pulled himself up out of the fresh water with a gasp. But Glen was already there, he wrapped his poncho around the man's face and clung it tight. The man staggered, pained by his blood loss and head trauma. He was going down. Glen just had to hang on.

The three doormen had reached Jock who was to the left of Tony. He slowly reached down to his belt where he had a dagger clipped. The men had tied Jock's feet, as they moved to his hands he pulled the hands that held his, down to his chest and crouched down, rolling one of the men over his back. With his free hands, he made a club and started braying down onto the man's face, which had landed just below him. Tony jumped up with the opportunity with his dagger in hand and launched it toward one of the standing men. He deflected the knife, that went over the top of Platty who had shuffled backwards to trip him. The other man came at Tony. He held a cricket bat which had been wrapped in razor wire. He swung it to Tony while moving quickly toward him. Tony's back hit a tree which stopped him retiring any further from the swinging razor wire. He ducked just in time to miss a fatal blow, and quickly spun around the trunk. The man swung from each side ripping fragments of bark from the side of the tree. Tony knew he couldn't run, the man would only use his team of prisoners, to lure him back. He had to put him down now. His dagger didn't have the length to get close to make any injury, he knew, his only option would be to throw it. He had only managed to hit a target a few times before by throwing a blade, but this one was moving, but this was the best shot he had.

He moved free from the trunk to set himself with an easier target. The man had slowed a little with the exhaustion of the weight of his modified weapon and resorted to threatening words, as opposed to swings. Tony took his advantage. He moved his grip to the tip of the blade and flicked it slightly higher, the weight would bring it lower to the man's torso. It spun fast then hit the man's bat and it flew away. The man laughed,

"YOU'RE FUCKED NOW YOU PIECE OF ..."

A stream of blood flowed down the side of the man's face. Its origin was a small metal disc that had imbedded into the side of his forehead. The man staggered back and lumbered down to all fours. Tony looked right, it was Glen who stood for a moment then ran toward Tony, throwing his knee into the man's face as he passed.

"Get down Tony" Glen whispered.

Jock had fought the best he could. His tied-up feet had made his movements clumsy and it didn't take long for him to be overpowered. He was rolled to his back while the man laid his fists into him. Platty had rolled on top of the man he had tripped and with Dunc and Donny they all got on top to keep the man down. The man thrashed and rolled to lift the dead weight, but he began to tire and slow.

"KEEP HIM DOWN!" Wilson had managed to edge free a little from his restraints. His wrists were bleeding from the rope burns but he was almost free. As Jock's attacker had weakened him enough, he stood again to see his man down. He ran to pull off the lads that lay on top of him. With his free hands, Wilson spotted a small knife, which had been dropped in the scuffle. He used it to cut his feet free, then quickly moved to Donny and freed his hands. He left the blade with him as his stood face to face with one of the doormen.

With no weapons and nothing left to lose, Wilson launched himself at the man. He was at least a foot shorter and 1/3 the size of his opponent but Bob Wilson was strong and fast. The last few days had put him through a lot. He didn't use that, he used the damage they had inflicted on his men. He didn't stop, he put everything he had left into bringing down his attacker. He didn't feel the punches to his face, nor the blows to his abdomen. If this was his last fight, he would go down winning it. It didn't matter if he ever recovered. All that mattered was that his men got out – and safe.

Donny had his hands free now and started working on his feet. Dunc had been thrown from his position and Platty was struggling with the task alone. He rushed down to cut Platty's hands free and as he did Platty was rolled off the doorman and landed on Donny. The man stood and his eyes bulged with his contempt. He raised his hand and pulled from its casing a broad sword he had under the back of his jacket.

Glen and Tony ran back towards the clearing. Wilson was further out in the woods fighting while Donny and Platty were locked in a defence against a broad sword. Dunc lay on the ground still bound but he has spotted a new radical to the already chaotic scene. A vehicle approached through the woods. It was going slow and steady, with is headlights off. The wind and rain had masked it sounds but it was heading for them. Glen looked to Tony,

"It looks like they've got reinforcements."

Their hearts sank. A new wave of foes wasn't making a win look possible. But they would not stop. Not until the final man fell. Glen pulled out two of his ninja stars, Tony was ready and held up his fists.

Donny and Platty were set backwards. The swings flew high and low. There was no break, their attacker had fresh adrenalin on his side. They moved further back opening more space between them, but the trees kept bringing their space back closer. Platty looked to Donny, he pointed forward. He was going to rush the swordsman. This wouldn't end well, but it would free Donny to make a claim to the weapon, but at the cost he felt was too high. He shook his head but Platty didn't meet his reply. The gap had been opened, but Platty moved to close it again. He prayed for good fortune, and that the blade wasn't as sharp as it looked. He took a final deep breath as he got ready to launch forward. But he never got the chance. Something stole his attack.

The jeep flew over the ground. It pounced over the uneven woodland floor and landed with enough momentum to roll forward. The swordsman was caught off guard from his reaper. The jeep pinned him against a large oak. He spat blood as he tried to push the impossible weight from his belly. His sword still held tightly in his hand, scraped and bounced off the jeep's bonnet. It slowly made its last strike and its wielder's face came to rest.

Denis stepped from the jeep and stood taking in the battleground.

"What the fuck, lads?"

The crash of the jeep stole Wilson's attention for a brief moment, as it did his opponent. Both men stood dangerously low on stamina. They panted hard, expelling large gusts of vapour as their heavy breaths met the cold air. The man saw the four soldiers exit the jeep. He looked back to Wilson and then started to run.

Wilson was exhausted, but he wouldn't let him escape. He ran faster and took the man's legs from the ground. He fell head first, and hard. Wilson was on his back and held him tight. He would pay for what he had done. The men he had tortured and killed. All the families he had ripped apart. Wilson fought his basic urge for revenge. He had to be bigger than this, he had to remain human and not become one of the savage monsters he had brought down.

30: Falling Reign

They sat around the campfire. It was raining hard but the canopy above them gave a dry shelter and their large team brought a security none had felt since entering the moors.

Denis, Grayson, Taff and Evo had secured all the prisoners. Two were dead, the other three unconscious. The jeep they had would have transported them out of the woods, that was if its possible engine damage from hitting the oak would allow it to move again. That seemed very unlikely. They would have to wait for Robert Tate to transport them out. The backup team had been freed from their shackles and grenade traps. Evo had buried the grenades for now marking their location on his map. Heaven knew if they were even real but none wanted to risk carrying any uncertain explosives.

The backup team had been through hell. They had entered the woods from the south twenty-four hours ago, and had been ambushed by three joined groups shortly after. They had put up a good fight, yet the numbers overpowered them and they were hung up and tortured until their radio was discovered. They had heard all the last days communications.

The backup team sat by the fire with their heads hung. They were exhausted and feeling responsible for the last attack. Glen and Jock had gathered some heather and added some to the fire. The rest they piled into a waterproof poncho to last the night. They sat and held their cold hands to the warm flames.

Wilson started looking at the doormen. Their hands and feet had been tied but he checked their injuries the best he could.

This was the first time any of the lads had taken any interest in their health, he was right to do so, as what they had done to the last lot, was not the way we had been brought up in the army. They were the enemy, yes, but when they are down and your prisoners they become a part of your responsibility. As much as you may not agree or care at all about them, it's the way you treat your prisoners of war, that is how you will be judged as people.

Half took watch while the others took time to rest. Morning was still hours away and the night reigned. For now, it was still and quiet, that was what everybody needed.

Kenny wasn't doing good, we were all soaked through and freezing. Our bodies had locked tightly into position to store what little body heat we had left. I had to push Brit to get himself on his feet and help me with Kenny. The rain had eased to a drizzle but the wind was so strong and kept the cold attacking our bones. We helped Kenny to his feet, he was like ice. He was shivering and his teeth chattering. All we could do was help him along. We re-fastened his coat and put his arms around our necks and set off looking for anywhere that would give us shelter. We could hardly see two feet in front of us. The wind was thrashing violently, we had to keep our heads down and just keep going. Kenny was heading towards hyperthermia; his lips were blue and his skin bright red and Brit wasn't far behind him.

We knew we couldn't go on anymore, Kenny kept falling to his knees and Brit was no longer able to support him.

They were giving up and I was close behind. I knew the lads were out there somewhere, but where the fuck were they? I had to do something, I wasn't going to fail Kenny and Brit, they had fallen down to their knees with exhaustion, with what little energy I had I scouted ahead a little. After another few metres, I spotted a small mound to the right of us. I felt the small spark of hope ignite. I ran back and nudged Brit and pulled up Kenny myself. I dragged him to the shelter of the mound while Brit stumbled behind us.

I lay Kenny in the underside, it was wet but sheltered from the wind. Brit tumbled under and fell next to Kenny. They both lay drifting in and out of consciousness. This wouldn't make them warm but at least the wind wouldn't make them any colder. I managed to get a clearer look of the area and spotted a rocky terrain around 50 metres away. I'd aim for those and look for any better shelter for us. "Hold tight boys, I'll not be long" They never acknowledged my words, they were out of it. I had to be quick, I had to get them out of this.

I set off the way we had come from. I checked to see if we had been followed. I could not see much, but if anyone was out there they would no doubt be taking shelter as well. I headed towards the rocks, my speed stunted by the wind forces before me, like invisible hands pushing my body away. I finally reached the summit, it looked to be the highest peak in the formation and stood around five metres high. I had a good view of the moorland where we had come across. I looked out to spot the mound where Kenny and Brit lay. The drizzle had stopped and the wind was still strong but beginning to ease. I ventured down the rocks looking for anything I could get the lads to. I spotted a small depression in the rock face with a large overhang above. It was perfect. We'd remain unseen here if we kept low. The path to reach the ledge was around thirty centimetres wide, only big enough to walk single file. It was what we needed for a defence but I worried how I'd manage to pull Kenny and Brit around this way. I'd been gone for nearly half an hour, it was time to get back to the lads.

The sun had welcomed me back to the moorland. It was bright but still absent of the heat we needed, but I was glad the wind and rain had all but gone. I climbed the slight accent then dropped down to my knees. There were figures across the moors, about one mile away, from the direction we had travelled overnight. I peered over and saw them rising and falling over the uneven ground. Brit and Kenny were around a hundred metres away. On the strangers next dip in the land I'd have to make a run for it, I'd only have a few seconds till they reemerged, but I'd have to take any opportunity I had to make it unseen. I ran. For all the anger and fear I felt, I ran.

Brit and Kenny still lay on top of each other. I shook Brit while keeping my fingers to my lips. His lips had returned to a more human shade but his face was pale. The movement woke Kenny and he painfully blinked to see what was going on. His eyelids were sticky and in the fresh light I could see his eyelashes had gelled together with discharge that I couldn't bare to contemplate right now.

"I've found somewhere to hide but we have to get there quickly, someone is coming."

The lads stood up slowly like men three times their age. Bones clicking back into life with every movement. I took a look over the mound, it looked clear but I waited in case the men were in one of the dips. They appeared but much further back this time, it looked an extra mile away. I felt relief, maybe we could wait here a little longer until they went completely out of sight? Kenny and Brit squatted looking to me for instruction. They looked more tired than ever, their pale and clammy skin, mottled with dirt made them look like zombies, they smelled like the undead as well, but I probably looked and smelled exactly the same. I rose up to take another look.

"*SHIT! FUCK!*" I ducked back down, there were two groups heading this way, about a mile each apart. The first appeared to be on solid flat ground now, there would be no more opportunity to move unseen.

We ran, as fast as we could, I led the way holding Kenny's hand. I knew he could barely see now and if he fell, we were dead. I didn't look back. It didn't matter now, we had to get to the ledge and pray we would not be spotted.

I led Kenny to the ledge first, I kept in front while using my right arm to steer him into the rocks. We made it in and I sat him at the back of the ledge. Brit had started coming along the path, he was more alert than Kenny but was unsteady on his feet, like he had snuck a couple of whiskeys in while I was away. I sat him next to Kenny and slid off his backpack. I left the studded branch for Brit and packed Kenny's blade. I knew he was too far gone to fight now, but I would use it to defend them. I stepped away to leave them and took one last look back. They sat huddled together with their eyes closed. The sun had started to get warmer and shone onto the ledge. Its sides reflected the heat inwards and set up a perfect incubator. I didn't know if I would see them again but I would do my best to save them.

I walked back to take a look from the top of the rocks. The grass along the small path was long and hadn't seen feet for a while; it sprang back up to attention. Hopefully it wouldn't look to anyone that it had been trodden on recently.

I reached the peak of the rocks and pulled off my pack, I laid out my bow and the five remaining arrows at two inches apart for easy loading. I rubbed Kenny's knife across the rock, sharpening it the best I could, and tucked it into my belt. I raised my head slowly; the hunters were approaching. Four jogged quickly about 500 metres away, the others about one mile behind.

Steadily, I took my bow and drew up an arrow. I was as ready as I ever could be. One way or another this was going to end.

31: The Alpha

04:00 hours hit and the rain had eased. The fire still burned
and the sun was starting to come through the heavily saturated
clouds. The land was waking up and its dawn chorus bore
its yawn. For Tony, Denis, Glen, Dunc, Donny and Wilson
the day had begun hours ago. They had already eaten their
rations, a bland oatmeal block with boiled water. Like the
taste in their mouths, they were ready for the final morning
in the moors. Their days prior had been relentless and tested
their bodies as well as minds. They felt that the fight so far
had been a learning curve. They had gone in assuming logic
and patterns, when really there were none. This was a game
and everyone's strategy had been different, defined by each
team's experience. They still had no idea where Geordie,
Kenny and Brit were. They had cut out some of their hunters
but still the danger remained. At least two teams were out
there and from Donny's infiltration intel, these had been out
here hunting many times before. If indeed they operated like
packs, these were the alpha teams. The fearless wolves, that
would never back down.

The two remaining teams had been the last to leave the
sheds. It stood to reason that this was not by accident. They
had let the inexperienced packs get ahead, while they watched
close by. They played with caution but the experience that
the prey, in this case especially, were far from the livestock
they had hunted before. They allowed the packs to thin out

before they moved in to steal the prize. The lads had been going after the wrong target. To find their men they had to find the alphas.

Ian and Robert had arrived at the moors during the night. They had parked the two vans two miles from the camp's location on an old farm road. It had felt good to be out in the field. Ian had held the mission at operations but he had been desperate to help out the lads in person. They had reached the camp and given all the latest information. By 04:00 hours all the prisoners had been taken to the vans, through the tireless wind and rain. They still had several left to pick up but they could not move across the moors just yet with doormen still out there.

By 05:00 all teams were stood with the vehicles. Ian and Robert would take the prisoners and the backup team back to base. It was time to face the music and report this back to the base R.S.M. and the authorities. Denis' interrogation with Billy had revealed more to what they all originally thought and now they had dead men's blood on their hands. This had moved beyond an off the record rescue to a mission with actual repercussions, involving official investigations and trials. Ian wanted to be there with his lads, he wanted to wipe away the last smile from the hunters' faces but he knew his skills of diplomacy and protocol were his objectives now.

They set off with the early morning sun for a journey that would change every man out there. Nothing would be the same again. Not after today.

The eleven-man team, set out together, they swept the land and they scouted. They had finally reached the end of the woods as the rain had lightened. Five men stood at the border searching through their binoculars. It was 06:50 and they were planning to move on. Jock hesitated, something had caught his attention. Something was flapping near the ground. It was low and was set in motion by the wind. A rain cover, he had assumed or maybe a piece of old tarp caught on a bush? He stood a moment longer. It disappeared and was replaced by a series of small lumps. They moved without the wind's force, this was something living. He kept his sight with it.

"We are moving out Jock, you coming?" Dunc didn't get a response so he moved closer to Jock and tapped him on the shoulder. Jock held up his hand and then returned it to his binoculars.

"There's eight men ahead. They are held up in a verge about two miles away." Jock didn't move, he was still like a statue. "They've spotted something. They are looking towards the rocks at three o'clock."

Dunc took out his binoculars. He found the same group. The men had separated, it looked like one group was heading to the top side of the rocks while the other was heading around the bottom. Dunc ran back to tell the rest of the lads while Jock stayed put. He watched them move across the moor slow at first and then they started to jog. They had found something and they were moving in.

32: All of Us

I stood at the precipice alone. It would end the way all things began. I couldn't believe this was how I would go down and I started to think of my family. They'd never know what happened to me. Never have a body to bury and never know the man I had become. I wanted tomorrow to come and for everything to be over. I'd overpowered eight men single handed, saved Kenny and Brit. My father would finally be proud of me and I'd walk back home with a new medal attached to my jacket. But that's not the reality tomorrow held. I knew this. The wilderness was the only thing that would know my fate, the sooner I let go of trying to prove my worth to anything other than myself, would I find my place in this. My measure, my worth wouldn't come from the end game. It came from the things I had done along the way.

I took my final look over the shield of rock I hid behind. The men were coming and had started walking up the steady incline to my location. I pulled my bow tight and raised up letting it fly. It flew over their heads unnoticed and bounced on the grass behind the last man. My face was sweating and my hands felt feeble as I loaded the second arrow. It flew faster than the first and sank into the stomach of the leading hunter. His eyes met mine as did the others. I didn't care anymore about running or hiding. This was it for me, my end. I loaded another arrow and set it free.

The man cradled the stick protruding his gut, it had

sunk a few centimetres into his flesh. The pain only sent his adrenalin into overdrive. He pulled the arrow out like it was nothing and threw it to the ground. His weapon, a gleaming sickle, moved forward, thirsty for action.

I moved further down the rock face. The four men close behind. I led them the opposite way from Kenny and Brit along another small pathway. It also had around a thirty centimetre berth. Up one side, a steep incline back to the moors, the other had a drop of at least twenty feet. I hadn't traversed this way so I was unsure how far I could go, but at least only one man could attack at a time. I was ten metres along before I turned, ready to face them. They stood still watching me go.

"Where's your friends gone then?" the leading man smirked.

"Long gone," I said. "It's just me now."

"Well here's the thing, we saw three of you run in here." He looked over the rocks and started to head backwards toward the ledge I'd left Kenny and Brit. "The other two didn't look too good, so I don't think they'll be that far away."

I edged forward, I couldn't let them reach the others, I needed them safe.

"I'll tell you what, I'll go and get their heads and I'll come back for yours. Give you a little head start to get running again." They turned and chanted as they went,

"RUN! RUN! RUN! RUN! RUN!"

My blood boiled and I ran, I ran up to the last man in the line. I buried Kenny's blade into his neck and kicked him down the cliff face. The next man turned and swung his bat at my head, I ducked and swung my blade at him. He dodged it but lost balance and started to fall down the drop, his hands grabbed the thick tufts of grass at the edge of the path. The next man in line laughed; he looked at his two fallen team and laughed loud and proud. He clapped and held his fists together. Each hand had a glove, one lined with thick wide studs and barbed wire, while the other had several pieces of serrated blades pierced through. Both covered in dried blood. He ran at me, I slid down low, taking away his feet. He stumbled over me and edged over the 20-metre drop. His heavy hand grabbed my left leg. The twisted wire tore into my thigh bringing me down. His body clashed with his friend trying to pull himself up on the grass, sending him tumbling down the rock face. He raised his bladed hand to strike at my head. I did the only thing I could. I let myself fall. The twisted barbed wire ripped through my thigh, my flesh tore wide on its exit, but the jagged rock face harmed my body the most. I bounced down the rocks four times, with each impact breaking my already broken body. I landed on my back unable to move. Unable to breathe. Every piece of air had been jettisoned from my lungs. I lay gasping like a fish out of water. And then it started again. The laughter, as twisted as his metal fist and as sick as the taste in my mouth. I was fucked.

I came to, unaware of space or time. Was I alive or dead? It took me a few moments to find reality again. I sat up and instantly regretted it. My head felt like a lead weight and judging from the dampness on my chest I knew my face was bleeding; I didn't feel it, I didn't want to know. I looked around and saw two bodies at the bottom with me. The man I had stabbed in the neck and the one with the bat, they lay with their eyes open. They were dead, the lunatic with the metal fists I couldn't see. I stood up an immediately vomited.

My throat and eyes burned like fire, but I shook it off and looked up to the pathway I had fallen from. No one was there.

'*SHIT! KENNY! BRIT!*' I looked for a way up the rock face but every step was agony, I couldn't climb up that way. I'd have to find a different way up to the ledge. I moved along the bottom of the cliff, the opposite side was steeper again, I had to settle with moving on the low ground. I kept looking up and forward. I had moved around 50 metres and could see the overhang of the ledge I had left the lads. There was no sound, no movement. They had gone. I had failed them!

Further ahead I could see a way up the cliff, it was steep but there were large, wide ledges that would make easy steps, were you a giant. I tried to raise my leg but the pain held me back. I tried to get my ass on it to lift myself up backwards but my arms could not support my weight. I rubbed my face in frustration and caught the fresh tears to my skin.

"*FUCK!*" I yelled aloud full of angst and pain, it echoed through the rock walls. I was done. I had failed them. I just wanted tomorrow to come. Tomorrow where this was over.

I heard his laughter again. It came from the direction I had just come from. I stood and reached for the blade in my belt, it wasn't there. It had been in my hand when I fell. It took nearly every bit of strength I had but I bent down and picked up a rock. I gripped it tight and waited. Two men came into view. The man I had shot with my arrow, his face was pale and his shirt bore the colour which should be under it, and the fucker with the gloves.

"You didn't get far did you!" one shouted angrily.

"I've been waiting for you to catch up," I said smugly and threw my rock as hard as I could. It skimmed the shoulder

of the gloved man. He laughed once more and ran at me.
A second rock hit him on top of his head. He stopped to
touch the blood that came from the wound. The rock hadn't
come from my hand. I turned and saw my brothers.

Kenny moved up close to me with the studded branch
while Brit moved past me with another few rocks in each
hand. He threw another, hitting the man behind just left of
his crotch. He moved backwards while Brit threw another. It
hit the gloved man in the mouth sending him to the ground.
Brit turned to me and smiled.

"We got this Geordie."

They ran up to the last men, Kenny kicked the laughing
fucker right in the face, he tossed the club over to Brit. He
caught it and moved forward to the last man. He held the
club high and as he let it fall he said something I would never
forget.

"Mess with him and *you mess with all of us.*"

My pride was unreal and the tears that had started to inflict
pain in my eyes, were worth it. They returned to my side and
I stood looking at them with a million words I wanted to say
to them. They never had the chance to leave my mouth. The
sound of clapping echoed the cliffs. We looked all around
us. Four men loomed over from the ledge above us.

"Good effort lads. That was the only other pack left in
the game." The four men stood tall. They were immaculate
and looked like they had just set foot in the moors.

"Your attempt was one of the best we've witnessed.
Don't worry, none of your men out here will get to see what
becomes of you. We got rid of your messages you left and
left them hunting the woods for you."

Brit just stared up at them. Kenny met my gaze. He knew,

like me, we couldn't fight anymore and Brit couldn't take them all on alone. But he would never give up. He picked up two rocks and placed one in my hand then moved in front of me.

"WE'RE NOT DONE YET YOU FUCKING DAFT PRICKS. COME ON DOWN HERE AND WE'LL SHOW YOU WHAT MAKES US BETTER THAN YOU BASTARDS!"

The men laughed at each other.

"And what's that then, *short stuff?*"

Kenny spat. I knew he'd make him regret calling him short.

"You mess with the army lads, you don't just get one of us…"

Three more men appeared above the ledge the men stood upon. Three more to their right and three more to their left while two joined us at its base.

"You get *all* of us," said Bob Wilson as he and Glen smacked down onto the ledge.

33: Tomorrow

We sat in warm jackets and hooded ponchos. It was the warmest I had felt for days. I sipped the cool water as the lads moved around before me. They moved their mouths but I couldn't hear a word that was spoken. The four hunters that had stood above us, were tied up at our feet. They screamed and resisted every touch made by our lads. But again, I didn't hear anything but my beating heart pulse through my ears. Brit was up chatting with Tony and Glen. They hugged and laughed while I sat there numb. I turned to Kenny. He was laid back on the rocks. His face looked to the sky with his mouth wide open taking in the fresh air.

I felt the air pressure change and I looked up, the noise of reality came flooding back in as a chopper flew overhead. As I lowered my head, I noticed Tony was stood in front of me. Tears started to roll down my face.

"Don't you cry, you big soft Geordie git. Or wait until you get a mirror, then you *will* cry, you look like shit mate." He smiled and I started to laugh. It was uncontrollable and pure.

Brit, Wilson and Denis joined me, Tony and Kenny at the rocks. "Good to have you back Geordie," Wilson said. "You were a little out of it when we found you."

"Sorry about that Bob, I've got a killer of a hangover."

Wilson smiled and told me what the lads had been through to find us. He told us of what Donny had gone through, Ian's backup team being caught and of what Denis had got from Billy. It made me feel like only a small cog in a very big wheel. We had all been through hell the last week, but still now the nightmare had never seemed closer to the world. It lurked just under the surface of real life and it terrified me. Wilson took hold of my shoulders.

"The R.S.M. has asked you be sent to base at Hereford. They'll get you back on the mend and then need a full briefing from you. A Q.R.F squad will need to talk with you. They will be interrogating all the captured doormen."

He took a deep breath, "The S.A.S. are now involved John. They are keeping this out of the public eye, for now, until they conduct their investigation."

"How big is this, Bob?" My question didn't have an answer. Wilson just stared at me. Two men ran up with a stretcher, Wilson turned and waved his hand to welcome their approach and then returned his eyes to mine,

"The chopper is ready for you now, Geordie. I'll see you soon."

My stretcher journeyed up through the cliff floor and returned up to the moors where the chopper sat. I could make out a lot of activity. Several choppers were grounded at various locations as far as I could see. Everything was getting a whitewash, nothing was being left to find. I saw one hovering over the woods and another some distance away, maybe over the sheds. I closed my eyes and left the moors behind.

As we came in to land at Hereford camp, I looked out of the open door on the side of the chopper. I could see a group of about twenty men on a field below waiting for us. There was an ambulance beside them as well as three Land Rovers. As soon as we touched down all the men ran to the chopper. They took me, Kenny and Brit straight to the camp hospital.

Me and Brit were in for six days while Kenny was in over a week. His eye was badly infected but luckily it was treatable. We felt like we told our story over one hundred times to a hundred different people. We never heard what information they had obtained from the doormen. Only that the investigation was still pending and a report would be issued soon. We all knew not to hold our breaths for that one.

We were pulled into one last meeting at Hereford base. The kind that took place in a hot room with low lights and several high-ranking S.A.S officers whose uniforms dripped with medals of prestige. Everything that had happened had not to be spoken about again. We were to stay at Hereford for the next week while investigations at our base were finalised.

Tony Glen and Dunc were the first permitted to come to the base to see us. God, we were glad to see them. The emotion that filled the room was unreal, I had never felt that level of it before. Tony came straight over to me and we hugged. I couldn't thank him enough.

"What are brothers for, mate?" he told me. At that we had more members in our family. The lads who had helped us at the moors we'd all be forever grateful to and we hoped one day we could repay them. Glen and Kenny picked up exactly where they left off. We laughed at Glen – the mother had finally been reunited with her long-lost son. We took the piss but we knew these emotions were real. I wasn't ashamed to tell the lads how I felt. Without them all I would not be here.

Kenny headed to Scunthorpe General at the end of the week. We knew he'd not be back to base for a while. He had a few setbacks in his treatment and they thought he may lose his eye.

After we got back to base, Bob Wilson got us all together. His words on parade had always been scripted but now they felt more real. He told us how proud he was of us. We had been tested in ways none of us could have thought possible and he was overwhelmed we had made it through together. He topped it off by saying we could all go back home the next day.

The morning of our departure we were called to Wilson's office. One S.A.S. officer sat in his room. Neither Brit or I had ever seen him before. He gave us an offer, one that changed our lives beyond any of our expectations. They wanted us to be part of a team to go deeper into the world of the hunters' circles. We'd have full access to equipment and resources and be fully compensated for our service. It was a world the police and S.A.S. could not go officially. Too much bureaucratic red tape. He digressed into trials and investigations which had run aground on similar cases and spun our heads with terms and protocols we felt too young and dumb to be privy to. His bottom line we understood. If we were caught by our legal system we would be prosecuted and sentenced like anybody else. We'd be seen as a few righteous squaddies who took justice into our own hands. They would take us out of the country for the sentence and wouldn't spend time in jail. We had one month to consider the offer, which would be extended to the others who had been out there with us.

After the meeting, we had been instructed to go to hangar one as well as the pay office; our heads still spinning from the information in our secret meeting.

Hangar one was amazing. As we walked in it had rows and rows of clothing, everything from socks, shirts to top coats. We had to take three sets of clothing and two pairs of shoes. At the end was a choice of all kinds of bags from hold-alls to cases, we couldn't believe it. From there we all headed to the pay office, we all got given £500 each and several letters that had arrived at the base for us. I stuffed the cash envelope in my bag and the single letter for me I folded into my trouser pocket.

We then headed out of the base to see a car waiting for us. Bob Wilson stood halfway between the car and us. He welcomed us with a smile. His body looked like it had fully recovered but his eyes told another story.

"The car will take you both to the train station lads. Enjoy your time back home." Wilson's smiled disappeared. "Think carefully about your next move lads. The S.A.S. want you all to be a part of this unit but it's a world some of us cannot join you in."

His words said more about his own involvement. I knew Wilson was dedicated to the army, but he also wanted to be a family man one day. He had served many years longer than us and this mission would take many more to come. I turned to Brit who was still looking to Wilson.

"Remember not to discuss this with anyone lads. This decision is yours to make alone." He shook each of our hands in turn. "I'll see you in two weeks." He nodded to us then headed back to base.

Me and Brit loaded ourselves into the car and it took us out of the base. It flew through the open countryside, miles of it. I looked out of the window seeing the wilderness with fresh eyes and a new understanding. Secrets lay under every leaf, danger in every chasm. I felt uncomfortable. I needed the world to belong to us again, not the darkness. Tomorrow wasn't a concept I felt I could use anymore. The wheels in motion were revolving today, getting through each moment couldn't rely on the hope of tomorrow only the here and now. I was ready. Me and the lads were ready, and I had made my decision.

At the station I knew Brit was still thinking hard. He shook my hand and voyaged off into the sea of travellers at the station without saying a word. I knew his mind wouldn't venture far from this moment over the next few weeks. I took my bag and headed through the station to find my platform. The noise and flow of people felt good; they existed in ignorance of who I was or what I had just been through. For the first time in weeks I felt unimportant and free.

I found my platform and I stood there, waiting by the tracks about to head home. The last few weeks seemed like it was someone else's journey. First the Falklands, then the hunt … now it was worse – *normality*. Could I really turn back and pretend to be normal for two weeks when I knew about the hunts, the packs and the men probably held in another shed on another hunting ground somewhere else? It made me feel empty yet restless. I had convinced myself that this new mission was what I needed to do, but I didn't share the confidence in the others in my unit. A warm gust of breeze lifted my head and brought with it a reminder that I needed to let go of it all for a while. Try to clear my head of everything and enjoy being home. I suddenly thought of meeting up with Dave McGlen again and it brought a smile back to my face.

The screeching rail tracks brought my train to my platform. I felt in my pockets for my tickets, they had fallen between the letter I had stuffed into my pocket back at the base. I took out the tickets and looked down at the envelope; it was plain white with my name printed on by a typewriter. I opened it and swallowed hard. I felt like I was right back in the moors again. My beating heart drummed harder and electricity fired up through my spine. The plain white sheet of paper had three markings on, crude symbols drawn by an even cruder hand, ones I had seen just over a week ago in the woods. Beneath them was a single word.

Run.

END OF PART ONE

Also by John Gordon
Part Two of Hell's Heroes

GOING DEEPER IN

Available Summer, 2021

ISBN: 978-1-78222-834-9